THE OLD SOUTH

Selected List of Other Books by Arna Bontemps

STORY OF THE NEGRO

WE HAVE TOMORROW

CHARIOT IN THE SKY

GOLDEN SLIPPERS *(Anthology)*

BLACK THUNDER

GOD SENDS SUNDAY

100 YEARS OF NEGRO FREEDOM

AMERICAN NEGRO POETRY *(Anthology)*

FAMOUS NEGRO ATHLETES

HOLD FAST TO DREAMS *(Anthology)*

GREAT SLAVE NARRATIVES *(Anthology)*

FREE AT LAST: *The Life of Frederick Douglass*

HARLEM RENAISSANCE REMEMBERED *(Editor)*

YOUNG BOOKER: *The Story of Booker T. Washington's Early Days*

With Jack Conroy

THE FAST SOONER HOUND

THEY SEEK A CITY

Edited by Langston Hughes and Arna Bontemps

THE BOOK OF NEGRO FOLKLORE

THE POETRY OF THE NEGRO (1746–1970)

THE
OLD SOUTH

"A Summer Tragedy" and Other Stories of the Thirties

ARNA BONTEMPS

DODD, MEAD & COMPANY
NEW YORK

A-1

ISBN: 0-396-06788-3
Library of Congress Catalog Card Number: 73-2136

Printed in the United States of America
by The Cornwall Press, Inc., Cornwall, N.Y.

CONTENTS

THE OLD SOUTH

WHY I RETURNED

The last time I visited Louisiana the house in which I was born was freshly painted. To my surprise, it seemed almost attractive. The present occupants, I learned, were a Negro minister and his family. Why I expected the place to be run down and the neighborhood decayed is not clear, but somewhere in my subconscious the notion had been planted and allowed to grow that rapid deterioration was inevitable where Negroes live. Moreover, familiar as I am with the gloomier aspects of living Jim Crow, this assumption did not appall me. I could reject the snide inferences. Seeing my birthplace again, however, after a considerable spread of years, I felt apologetic on other grounds.

Mine had not been the varmint-infested childhood so often the hallmark of Negro American autobiography. My parents and grandparents had been well-fed, well-clothed, and well-housed. One does not speak of ancestors who lived publicly—Creole style—with their colored families and gave proof of fealty to dark offspring. Some have called these genealogies unwritten history. I have come to feel that mine was fairly typical. I observe with more than mild surmise, for example, that all the Negroes in the Congress bear the mark of a similar tradition, that many faces conspicuous in government, in the United Nations, even among the Black Muslims, are so obviously of mixed ancestry that the bald expurgation of this fact from the history of the South becomes increasingly comical. The cold—or hot—fact is that down here there is a widespread kinship, sometimes unknown, generally unacknowledged. There are old folks from my home who say, knowing something about the background of the city, they would bet a hatful of money that some of those "white" women seen on television hooting and poking out their tongues and spitting at Negro children integrating New Orleans public schools a year or two ago were themselves as colored as Adam Clayton Powell. In any case, the Civil War and the violent disorders that followed Reconstruction tended to restrict, if they did not immediately end, such quaint companionship, so my birthplace was only indirectly connected with it.

In my earliest recollections of the corner at Ninth and Winn both streets were rutted and sloppy. On Winn there was an abominable ditch where water settled for weeks at a time. I can remember Crazy George, the town idiot, following a flock of geese with the bough of a tree in his hand, standing in slush while the geese paddled about or probed into the muck. So fascinated was I, in fact, that I did not hear my grandmother calling from the kitchen door.

It was after I felt her hand on my shoulder shaking me out of my daydream that I trumped up the absurdity that made her laugh. "You called me Arna," I protested, when she insisted on knowing why I had not answered. "My name is George." And so it became, where she was concerned, for the rest of her years.

I had already become aware of nicknames among the people we regarded as members of the family. Teel, Mousie, Buddy, Pinkie, Ya-ya, Mat, and Pig all had other names which one heard occasionally. Even the dog Major had a nickname. The homefolks called him Coonie. I got the impression that to be loved intensely one needed a nickname. My mother preferred to call these pet names, and I was glad my grandmother, whose love mattered so much, had found one she liked for me, *George*.

My hand was in hers a good part of the time, as I recall. If we were not decorating a backyard bush with egg shells, for my young uncles to come home from school, we were under the tree in the front yard picking up pecans after one of the boys had climbed up and shaken the branches. If we were not decorating a backyard bush with egg shells, we were driving in our buggy across the bridge to Pineville on the other side of the Red River. I never found out whether or not the horse had any name other than Daisy.

The serenity of my grandmother in those days was recognized by many who knew her, but it took me a number of years to find out what made it seem remarkable. All I knew then was that this idyll came to a sudden and senseless end at a time when everything about it seemed flawless. In one afternoon scene, my mother and her several sisters had come out of their sewing room with thimbles still on their fingers, needles and thread stuck to their tiny aprons, and were filling their pockets with pecans. Next, it seemed, we were at the railroad station catching a train, my mother, my sister, and I, with a young woman named Sousie.

The story behind it, I learned, concerned my father. His vague presence had never been with us under the pecan tree or on our buggy rides. When he was not away working at brick or stone construction, other things occupied his time. He had come from a family of builders. His oldest brother had married into the Metoyer family on Cane River, descendants of the free Negroes who were the original builders of the famous Melrose plantation mansion. Another brother older than my father went down to New Orleans, where his daughter married one of the prominent jazzmen. My father was a band man himself, and, when he was not working too far away, the chances were he would be blowing his horn under the direction of Claiborne Williams, whose passion for band music awakened the impulse that worked its way down the river and helped to quicken American popular music.

In appearance my father was one of those dark Negroes with "good" hair—meaning almost straight. This did not bother anybody in Avoyelles parish, where the type was common and "broken French" accents were expected, but later in California people who had traveled in the far East wondered if he were not a Ceylonese or something equally exotic. In Alexandria, Louisiana, his looks, good clothes, and hauteur seem to have been something of a disadvantage in the first decade of this century.

Returning home one Saturday night after collecting his pay and spending a part of it on presents for his wife and youngsters, he was walking on Lee Street when two white men wavered out of a saloon and blocked his path. One of them muttered sloppily, "Let's walk over the big nigger."

Frozen for a moment, my father felt his muscles knot. Inside the saloon the voices also sounded strangely belligerent. Was something brewing? Racial tension again? The two men on the sidewalk were unimportant. He was not afraid of their threat. But was this the time or place for a showdown? Assuming he could handle them two-on-one, what then? For striking a white man the routine penalty was mob vengeance, regardless of the provocation. Had a family man a right to sell his pride, or even his honor, in this way at the expense of his dependents? He was capable of fury, and he might have reasoned differently at another time, but that night he calmly stepped aside, allowing the pair to have the walk to themselves. The decision he made as he walked the remaining blocks to our home changed everything for all of us.

My first clear memory of him as a person was the picture he made standing outside the Southern Pacific Depot in Los Angeles. He was shy about showing emotion—he often seemed blunt—so he greeted us quickly on our arrival and let us know this was the place he had chosen for us to end our journey. We had tickets to San Francisco and were prepared to continue beyond if necessary.

We moved into a house in a neighborhood where we were the only colored family. The people next door and up and down the block were friendly and talkative, the weather was perfect, there wasn't a mud puddle anywhere, and my mother seemed to float about on the clean air. When my grandmother and a host of other relatives followed us to this refreshing new country, I began to pick up comment about the place we had left, comment which had been withheld from young ears while we were still in Louisiana.

For one thing they mentioned the house my father had just started building in Alexandria when he decided to drop everything and make his move. They talked about Joe Ward, my grandmother's younger brother, nicknamed Buddy. I could not remember seeing him in Louisiana, and I now learned he had been down at the Keeley Institute in New Orleans taking a cure for alcoholism. A framed portrait of Buddy was placed in my grandmother's living room in California. It pictured a young mulatto dandy with an elegant cravat and jewelled stickpin. All the talk about him gave me an impression of style, grace, éclat.

All of that was gone a few years later, however, when we gathered to wait for him in my grandmother's house and he entered wearing a detachable collar without a tie and did not remove his hat. His clothes did not fit. They had been slept in for nearly a week on the train. His shoes had come unlaced. His face was pock-marked. Nothing in his appearance resembled the picture in the living room.

Two things redeemed the occasion, however. He opened his makeshift luggage and brought out jars of syrup, bags of candy my grandmother had said in her letters that she missed, pecans, plus filet for making gumbo. He had stuffed his suitcase with these instead of clothes. He had not brought an overcoat or a change of underwear. As we lit into the sweets, he began to talk, and I became entranced. He was not trying to impress or even entertain. He was just telling how things were down home, how he had not taken a drink or been locked up since he came back from Keeley the last time, how the family of his employer and benefactor had been scattered or died, how the schoolteacher friend of the family, Mr. George O' Quano, was getting along, how high the Red River had risen along the levee, and such things.

Someone mentioned his employer's daughter. A rumor persisted that Buddy once had a dangerous crush on her. This, I took it, had to be back in the days when the picture in the living room was made. It was all mostly gossip, he commented with only a shadow of a smile. Never had been much to it, and it was too long ago to talk about now. He did acknowledge, significantly, I thought, that his boss's daughter had been responsible for his enjoyment of poetry and novel reading and had taught him perhaps a thousand songs, but neither of these circumstances had undermined his lifelong employment in her father's bakery, where his specialty was fancy cakes. Buddy had never married. Neither had the girl.

The dim rumor of interracial romance had an air of unreality, but it prompted one of my aunts to tell me later something Buddy had told her in confidence. One of the sons of Buddy's boss appeared to have strong feelings against Negroes. When this young man got married and brought a beautiful brunet wife home from New Orleans, some of his cronies taunted him by saying she looked as if she might have a drop or two of colored blood. He appeared to laugh it off, but Buddy found out that the boss's son promptly returned to New Orleans and hired an investigator to look up the records and find out whether there was anything to the innuendo about his bride. After a careful search the investigator reported cheerfully that her pedigree was clear: she had no Negro blood. However, in the course of his research, the investigator had found that the young husband *did,* on his mother's side. And this discovery, Buddy revealed, was the explanation of the young man's subsequent suicide, which publicly had remained a mystery.

When my mother became ill, a year or so after Buddy's arrival, we went to live with my grandmother in the country for a time. Buddy was there. He had acquired a kind of rusticity wholly foreign to his upbringing. Never before had he worked outdoors. Smoking a corncob pipe and wearing oversized clothes provided by my uncles, he resembled a scarecrow in the garden, but the dry air and the smell of green vegetables seemed to be good for him. Perhaps they were continuing the restoration begun at the Keeley Institute. In any case, I promptly became his companion and confidant in the corn rows.

At mealtime we were occasionally joined by my father, home from his bricklaying. The two men eyed each other with suspicion, but they did not quarrel immediately. Mostly they reminisced about Louisiana. My father would say, summarizing now and then, "Sometimes I miss all that. If I was just thinking about myself, I might want to go back and try it again. But I've got the children to think about—their education."

"Folks talk a lot about California," Buddy would reply

thoughtfully, "but I'd a heap rather be down home than here, if it wasn't for the conditions."

Obviously their remarks made sense to each other, but they left me with a deepening question. Why was this exchange repeated after so many of their conversations? What was it that made the South—excusing what Buddy called the *conditions*—so appealing. Was it the same thing that made my father determined to keep his children away from it? Was this a lust, a craving, a kind of illicit love they were feeling?

There was less accord between them in the attitudes they revealed when each of the men talked to me privately. My father respected Buddy's ability to quote the whole of Thomas Hood's "The Vision of Eugene Aram," praised his reading and spelling ability, but he was concerned, almost troubled, about the possibility of my adopting the little old derelict as an example. He was horrified by Buddy's casual and frequent use of the word *nigger*. Buddy even forgot and used it in the presence of white people once or twice that year, and was soundly criticized for it. Buddy's new friends, moreover, were sometimes below the level of polite respect. They were not bad people. They were what my father described as don't-care folk. To top it all, Buddy was still crazy about the minstrel shows and minstrel talk that had been the joy of his young manhood. He loved dialect stories, preacher stories, ghost stories, slave and master stories. He half-believed in signs and charms and mumbo jumbo, and he believed wholeheartedly in ghosts.

When I told him on the authority of my schoolteachers that there were no such things as ghosts, he sneered,

"That's pure nonsense. I seen one just last night. He was standing up yonder by the gate." He went on after that to recall hundreds of encounters he had had with ghosts since his childhood.

My father's opinion was that Buddy had probably been drunk when he saw most of them, and hence these did not count as authentic experiences. For the rest, my father had picked up in California an explanation about ghosts that I found even more dreadful than Buddy's amused acceptance of hants. Someone had proved to my father from the Bible that the devil could change himself into an angel of light and appear to people in various guises. This is what "ignorant" people were actually seeing when they thought they saw ghosts. He believed this "fact" should dispose of Buddy's "old fogy-ism." Whether it did or not, it nearly scared me to death.

I took it that my father was still endeavoring to counter Buddy's baneful influence when he sent me away to a white boarding school during my high school years, after my mother had died. "Now don't go up there acting colored," he cautioned. I believe I carried out his wish. He sometimes threatened to pull me out of school and let me scuffle for myself the minute I fell short in any one of several ways he indicated. He never did. But before I finished college, I had begun to feel that in some large and mighty important areas I was being miseducated, that perhaps I should have rebelled.

How dare anyone—parent, schoolteacher, or merely literary critic—tell me not to act *colored*. White people have been enjoying the privilege of acting like Negroes for more than a hundred years. The minstrel show, the most popular form of entertainment in America for a whole generation, simply epitomized, while it exaggerated, this privilege. Today nearly everyone who goes on a dance floor starts acting colored immediately, and this has been going on since the cake walk was picked up from Negroes and became the rage. Why should I be ashamed of such influences? In popular music, as in the music of religious fervor, there is a style that is unmistakable, and its origin is certainly no mystery. On the playing field a Willy Mays could be detected by the way he catches a ball, even if his face were hidden. Should the way some Negroes walk be changed or emulated? Sometimes it is possible to tell whether or not a cook is a Negro without going into the kitchen. How about this?

In their opposing attitudes toward roots my father and my great-uncle made me aware of a conflict in which every educated American Negro, and some who are not educated, must somehow take sides. By implication at least, one group advocates embracing the riches of the folk heritage; their opposites demand a clean break with the past and all it represents. Had I not gone home summers and hobnobbed with folk-type Negroes, I would have finished college without knowing that any Negro other than Paul Laurence Dunbar ever wrote a poem. I would have come out imagining that the story of the Negro could be told in two short paragraphs: a statement about jungle people in Africa and an equally brief account of the slavery issue in American history. The reserves of human vitality that enabled the race to survive the worst of both these experiences while at the same time making contributions to western culture remained a dark secret with my teachers, if they had considered the matter at all. I was given no inkling by them, and my white classmates who needed to know such things as much as I did if we were to maintain a healthy regard for each other in the future, were similarly denied.

So what did one do after concluding that for him a break with the past and the shedding of his Negro-ness were not only impossible but unthinkable? First, perhaps, he went to New York in the twenties, met young Negro writers and intellectuals who were similarly searching, learned poems like Claude McKay's "Harlem Dancer" and Jean Toomer's "Song of the Son," started writing and publishing in this vein himself, and applauded Langston Hughes when he wrote in the *Nation* in 1926:

> We younger Negro artists who create now intend to express our individual dark-skinned selves without fear or shame. If white people are pleased we are glad. If they are not, it doesn't matter. We know we are beautiful. And ugly too. The tom-tom cries and the tom-tom laughs. If colored people are pleased we are glad. If they are not, their displeasure doesn't matter either. We build our temples for tomorrow, strong as we know how, and we stand on top of the mountain free within ourselves.

At least that was how it was with me. My first book was published just after the depression struck. Buddy was in it—conspicuously—and I sent him a copy, which I imagine he read. In any case, he took the occasion to celebrate. Returning from an evening with his don't-care friends, he wavered along the highway and was struck by an automobile. He was sixty-seven, I believe.

Alfred Harcourt, Sr., was my publisher. When he invited me to his office, I found that he was also to be my editor. He explained with a smile that he was back on the job doing editorial work because of the hard times. I soon found out what he meant. Book business appeared to be as bad as every other kind, and the lively and talented young people I had met in Harlem were scurrying to whatever brier patches they could find. I found one in Alabama.

It was the best of times and the worst of times to run to that state for refuge. Best, because the summer air was so laden with honeysuckle and spiraea it almost drugged the senses at night. I have occasionally returned since then but never at a time when the green of trees, of countryside, or even of swamps seemed half so wanton. While paying jobs were harder to find there than in New York—indeed they scarcely existed—one did not see evidences of hunger. Negro girls worked in kitchens not for wages but for the toting privilege, that is, permission to take home leftovers.

Meanwhile, the men and boys rediscovered woods and swamps and streams with which their ancestors had been intimate a century earlier and about which their grandparents still talked wistfully. The living critters still abounded. They were as wild and numerous as anybody had ever dreamed; some small, some edible, some monstrous. I made friends with these people, heard their dogs at night, and went with them on possum hunts. I was astonished to learn how much game they could bring home without gunpowder, which they did not have. When the possum was treed by the dogs, a small boy went up and shook him off the limb and the bigger fellows finished him off with sticks. Nets and traps would do for birds and fish. Cottontail rabbits driven into a clearing were actually run down and caught by barefoot boys. These were prized no more, however, than the delicious mushrooms which hunters and housewives had recently learned to distinguish from the poisonous variety. The locations of the best fruit- and nut-bearing trees in the woods were kept as choice secrets by their discoverers.

Such carrying-on amused them while it delighted their palates. It also took their minds off the hard times, and they were ready for church when Sunday came. I followed them there, too, and soon began to understand why they enjoyed it so much. The preaching called to mind James Weldon Johnson's "The Creation" and "Go Down Death." The long-meter singing was from another world; the shouting was ecstasy itself. At a primitive Baptist foot-washing I saw benchwalking for the first time, and it left me breathless. The young woman who rose from her seat and skimmed from the front of the church to the back, her wet feet lightly touching the tops of the pews, her eyes upward, could have astounded me no more had she walked on water. The members fluttered and wailed, rocked the church with their singing, and accepted the miracle for what it was.

We lived in a decaying plantation mansion for a time, entertaining its ghosts in our awkward way. An ancient visitor from a snug little community folded between nearby hills came to call and told us that in his boyhood older folks often talked about Andrew Jackson's visits with the first occupants of the house. Later we moved into a tiny new cottage a stone's throw from an abandoned sawmill and within hollering distance of a wooded swamp. Night and morning we were aroused by sounds of bedlam among its flying, creeping, or climbing inhabitants. I set up my portable typewriter on the shady side of the cottage and began writing such children's stories as *You Can't Pet a Possum* and *Sad-Faced Boy*.

It was the worst time to be in northern Alabama because the big road between Huntsville and the Tennessee line was unpaved, rutted, and hard to traverse. If you came down from Nashville at night, pushing your little secondhand Ford briskly, you ran off the pavement with a jolt and automatically yelled "Bam!" That was also the year of the trials of the nine Scottsboro boys in nearby Decatur. Instead of chasing possums at night and swimming in creeks in the daytime, this bunch of kids without jobs and nothing else to do had taken to riding empty box cars. When they found themselves in one with two white girls wearing overalls and traveling the same way, they did not have to be told they were in bad trouble. The charge against them was rape, and the usual verdict in Alabama, when a Negro man was so much as remotely suspected, was guilty; the usual penalty, death. Several times I was tempted to go over and try my luck at getting through the crowds and into the courtroom to hear the trials. My wife did not favor this, and neither did I on second thought. We were not transients, as were most of the spectators, and that made a difference. The ghosts in the old mansion and the screams in the swamp were about as much of the horror as we could cope with while at the same time trying to write a little when the spirit moved.

To relieve the tension while we waited for a verdict, we

drove to Athens one night and listened to a program of music by young people from Negro high schools and colleges in the area. A visitor arrived from Decatur during the intermission and reported shocking developments at the trial that day. Ruby Bates, one of the girls involved, had given testimony about herself that reasonably should have taken the onus from the boys. It had only succeeded in infuriating the throng around the courthouse. The rumor that reached Athens was that crowds were spilling along the highway, lurking in unseemly places, whispering, and threatening to vent their anger. After the music was over, someone suggested nervously that those of us from around Huntsville leave at the same time, keep our cars close together as we drove home, and be prepared to stand by, possibly help, if anyone met with mischief.

We readily agreed. Though the drive home was actually uneventful, the tension remained and I began to take stock with a seriousness comparable to my father's when he stepped aside for the Saturday night bullies on Lee Street in Alexandria. I was younger than he had been when he made his move, but my family was already larger by one. Moreover, I had weathered a northern as well as a southern exposure. My education was different, and what I was reading in newspapers differed greatly from anything he could have found in the Alexandria *Town Talk* in the early 1900s.

With Gandhi making world news in India while the Scottsboro case inflamed passions in Alabama and awakened consciences elsewhere, there was less inclination for me than there had been for him to restrict my thoughts to my personal situation. I could see, as I thought, something beginning to shape up, possibly something on a wide scale. As a matter of fact, I had already written a stanza foreshadowing the application of a nonviolent strategy to the Negro's efforts in the South:

> We are not come to wage a strife
> With swords upon this hill;
> It is not wise to waste the life
> Against a stubborn will.
> Yet would we die as some have done:
> Beating a way for the rising sun.

Even so, deliverance did not yet seem imminent, and it was becoming plain that an able-bodied young Negro with a healthy young family could not continue to keep friends in that community if he sat around trifling with a typewriter on the shady side of his house when he should have been working or at least digging in the yard and trying to raise something for the table. Luckily the tires on the Ford were almost new, and there was nothing wrong with the motor. I decided that this would be a good time to see what it would do on the road.

We did not learn till later (when I read *The Grapes of Wrath*) who all those people were that we saw headed for California as we went. Nor did we fall among them out there. We visited with my kinfolks, acquainted my old friends with our youngsters, and boarded with my father and stepmother till I could finish a book, collect an advance, sell the Ford, and move on to Chicago.

Crime seemed to be the principal occupation of the South Side at the time of our arrival. The openness of it so startled us that we could scarcely believe what we saw. In a few months my feeling ran from revulsion to despair.

Twice our small apartment was burglarized. Nearly every week we witnessed a stick-up, a purse-snatching or something equally dismaying on the street. Once I saw two men get out of a car, enter one of those blinded shops around the corner from us, return dragging a resisting victim, slam him into the back seat of the car, and speed away. We had fled from the jungle of Alabama's Scottsboro area to the jungle of Chicago's crime-ridden South Side, and one was as terrifying as the other.

I woke from these nightmares and began dreaming of a beachcomber's island, complete with mango tree and thatched hut. A summer trip to the Caribbean, made possible by a fellowship grant, may have abetted the fantasy, but it also convinced me that my only real option was to continue racking my brain.

Despite literary encouragement, the heartiness of a writing clan that adopted me and bolstered my courage, and a gradual adjustment to the rigors of the depression, I never felt I could settle permanently with my family in Chicago. I could not accept the ghetto, and ironclad residential restrictions against Negroes situated as we were made escape impossible. Thus we were confined to neighborhoods where we had to fly home each evening before darkness fell and honest people abandoned the streets to predators. Garbage was dumped in alleys around us. Police protection was regarded as a farce. Corruption was everywhere.

A precinct worker promised that if we registered to vote, we would receive Christmas boxes for the children. We registered, since she represented the party of our choice, and tried to forget the implications of that second remark.

We were astonished not only that she kept her word but that the boxes she showed up with were so large and contained clothes of such excellent quality. We learned later that these boxes had been prepared for the "needy" and went to those who had registered as we had been advised. When I inquired about transfers for two of our children to integrated schools more accessible to our address, I was referred to a person not connected with the school system or the city government. He assured me he could arrange the transfers—at an outrageous price. These represented ways in which Negro leadership was operating in the community at that time and how it had been reduced to impotence.

I did not consider exchanging this way of life for the institutionalized assault on Negro personality one encountered in the Alabama of the Scottsboro trials, but suddenly the campus of a Negro college I had twice visited in Tennessee began to seem attractive—somewhat of a prose equivalent of that beachcomber's island. There, one should be able to relax at least enough to entertain his own thoughts. A measure of isolation, a degree of security seemed possible. If a refuge for the harassed Negro could be found anywhere in those days, it had to be in such a setting. If there was any way to count on higher educational opportunities for a family growing as fast as mine, this appeared to be it.

Even so, waiting on a beach—a temporary expedient—is one thing; settling down for the best years of one's life is another. We had made the move, and I had become the Librarian at Fisk University when a series of train trips during World War II gave me an opportunity for reflections of another kind. I started making notes for an essay to be called "Thoughts in a Jim Crow Car." Before I could finish it, Supreme Court action removed the curtains in the railway diners, and the essay lost its point. While I had been examining my own feelings and trying to understand the need men have for such customs, the pattern had altered. Compliance followed with what struck me, surprisingly, as an attitude of relief by all concerned. White passengers, some of whom I recognized by their positions in the public life of Nashville, who had been in the habit of maintaining a frozen silence until the train crossed the Ohio River, now nodded and began chatting before it left the Nashville station. I wanted to stand up and cheer. I did not, of course, and when on the same impulse the Army began to desegregate its units, I was sure I detected fatal weakness in our enemy. Segregation, the monster that had terrorized my parents and driven them out of the green Eden in which they had been born, was itself vulnerable and could be attacked, possibly destroyed. I felt as if I had witnessed the first act of a spectacular drama. That I would want to stay around for the second went without saying.

Without the miseries of segregation, the South as a homeplace for a Negro of my temperament had clear advantages. In deciding to wait and see how it worked out, I was also betting that progress toward this objective would be more rapid in the southern region, and the results more satisfying than could be expected in the metropolitan centers of the North where whites were leaving the crumbling central areas to Negroes while they themselves moved into restricted suburbs and began setting up another kind of closed society.

Down here, in addition to the fact that some of us are unrecognized kin, we know each other pretty well. We know more about each other then we tell. During slavery, the South filled this country with mulattoes much as the Snopes family filled the Faulkner country with spotted horses. Working with Negroes in some relationship or other is part of the experience of nearly every Southerner and, with many, cooperation on higher levels is nothing new. Will Alexander told me in 1943 that he was convinced the South was ready to settle the race problem for fifty cents on the dollar. As a dyed-in-the-wool southern liberal, however, he was not recommending that Negroes should be enticed by such a deal. He favored holding out for one hundred cents on the dollar, if that was the way to put it.

Many Negroes owned property close to the finest white residences under the old regime. Apparently the southern gentry felt more secure with Negroes nearby. The idea that Negroes devaluated the property was one of the carpetbaggers' swindles. The change came as the upper class whites, like the European aristocracy, became ineffective. The Negro lost his place and security as the middle class assumed dominance. Nevertheless, many white southerners continue to have Negro neighbors, as some had always had, and complaints are seldom heard on this score.

Segregation as a racket promoted by carpetbaggers found ready adherents, of course, because of the ways in which it lent itself to the economic squeeze. Banks, real estate operators, insurance companies, politicians, and many others found ruses by which to make it turn an unrighteous profit. Few but the ignorant or the naïve could have believed deeply that the practice was moral, and certainly none of the people with whom I have been associated have ever been willing to compromise on this principle. We were and are here to oppose segregation and try in every way to undermine it. Charles S. Johnson had this continuing effort in mind, no doubt, when he talked about "intensive minority living."

The second act of the spectacular on which I had focused began with the 1954 decision of the Supreme Court that cut down the old separate but equal façade behind which inequality was perpetuated. While this was a landmark, it provoked no wild optimism. I had no doubt that the tide would now turn, but it was not until the freedom movement began to press itself that I felt reassured. We were in the middle of it in Nashville. Our little world commenced to sway and rock with the fury of a resurrection. I tried to discover just what it was that made it shake, how the energy was generated. I think I found it.

The singing that broke out in the ranks of protest marchers, in the jails where sit-in demonstrators were held, and in the mass meetings and boycott rallies, was gloriously appropriate. The only American songs suitable for a resurrection—or a revolution, for that matter—are Negro spirituals. The surge these awakened was so mighty it threatened to change the name of our era from the "space age" to the "age of freedom."

Some literary work appeared in the course of these events, and there were those who thought that travail such as this called for a latter day Thomas Paine. In the North a clutch of sensational books, plays, and magazine pieces profited from the foment, perhaps, but they were irrelevant to the movement itself. The momentum of the marchers came from the sermons of Martin Luther King, Jr., and his cohorts. The lineage of this king of expression is well-known to devotees of Negro folk preaching. It has its own style. Evoking audience response and participation, it is not unrelated to the call and response pattern of some Negro spirituals—a pattern which scholars have traced to Africa.

One was obliged to notice that Negroes in the South seemed better armed for a struggle with spiritual overtones than their kinfolk in the North. I suspected, and I still believe, that they are less likely to go berserk than the Harlemites. Willing to sacrifice, even to take risks, they are more apt to keep their cool, as the college kids say. Perhaps the word is morale. Moreover, you can communicate with them because you know where to find them. Often that will be in church—a good place for them to catch the beat of the call and response and slip in a hot lick now and then during the gospel singing.

The southern Negro's link with his past seems to me worth preserving. His greater pride in being himself, I would say, is all to the good, and I think I detect a growing nostalgia for these virtues in the speech of relatives in the North. They talk a great deal about "Soulville" nowadays, when they mean "South." "Soulbrothers" are simply the homefolks. "Soulfood" includes black-eyed peas, chitterlings, grits and gravy, and all are held in the warmest esteem. Aritha Franklin, originally from Memphis, sings, "Soulfood—it'll make you limber; it'll make you quick."

Needless to say, vacations in Soulville by these expatriates in the North tend to become more frequent and to last longer since times began to get better.

I was interested a year or so ago in a tiff between a group of militant Negro intellectuals in New York and "white liberals." It was not clear to me just who constituted the group under attack, but I assumed the others were really disturbed by what they saw as hypocrisy. Of course, hypocrisy is everybody's affliction, and its presence in race relations could become a problem in the South at a future time. At present, however, the southern situation does not lend itself to hypocrisy of this kind. Some Negroes in personal service may have retained attitudes traditional to that occupation, but southern whites, alas, do not yet have enough incentive to feign liberality when they do not feel it. A greater problem at this stage is the encouragement of timid liberals whose hearts are on the right side to stand up and be counted.

Colleagues of mine at Fisk University who, like me, have pondered the question of staying or going have sometimes given other reasons. The effective young dean of the Chapel, for example, who since has been wooed away by Union Theological Seminary, felt constrained mainly by the opportunities he had here to guide a large number of students and by the privilege of identifying with them. John W. Work, the musicologist and composer, found the cultural environment more stimulating than any available to him in the North. Aaron Douglas, an Art professor, came down thirty-odd years ago to get a "real, concrete experience of the touch and feel of the South." Looking back, he reflects, "If one could discount the sadness, the misery, the near volcanic intensity of Negro life in most of the South and concentrate on the mild almost tropical climate and the beauty of the landscape, one is often tempted to forget the senseless cruelty and inhumanity the strong too often inflict on the weak."

For my own part, I am staying on in the South to write something about the Negro's awakening and regeneration. That is my theme, and this is where the main action is. Also, there is this spectacular I'm watching. Was a climax reached with the passage of the Civil Rights Act of 1954, or was it with Martin Luther King's addressing Lyndon B. Johnson as "my fellow Southerner?" In any case, having stayed this long, it would be absurd not to wait for the third act.

THE CURE

He always told his dream at the breakfast table, and this one was not unlike the others.

"Maw came back to me last night," he began, his lids fluttering over watery eyes marred by cataracts. "She was standing on the piazza with a long stick in her hand and she was calling me so loud I could still hear her voice after it woke me up. Then I knew it wasn't a piazza she was standing on because we haven't got a piazza here like we had down home in Louisiana. She was standing out there in the yard by the pump and shaking one of them willow switches at me."

My grandmother didn't want to hear any more. She rose abruptly and walked over to the kitchen window with cup and saucer in her hands.

"That old whiskey you been drinking—that's all."

Buddy Joe Ward wasn't offended. He took her remark not as a reproach, but simply as a statement—and not a very enlightened one. When he looked at me, his smile showed an indulgence for his older sister that he expected me to understand.

"She was aiming to beat me, Maw was. One thing about Maw: she believed in the rod. Didn't make no difference how old you was, Maw would lay it on if you needed it. I was a grown man, talking about getting married, last time Maw whipped me."

Grandma kept her eyes fixed on the sugar beet fields behind our house on Alameda Road and on the cattail swamps beyond.

"You was grown, but you wasn't no man," she corrected.

Again Buddy gave me his smile and nod. This older sister had been looking after him since before Maw died; she was still looking after him, and he owed her a certain deference, but this did not require him to answer all her nonsense. He waited a moment and then went on as if he had not been interrupted.

"I came in the house kind of late that time. I'd been drinking and maybe my clothes was mussed up."

"No such a thing." Grandma lost her patience. "It was the next day. You'd been in jail. The police picked you up, and Mr. O'Shea had to go down in the morning and get you out. When four o'clock came and you wasn't in the bakery getting the bread started, he knew right where to go. It was after breakfast when you came home to change up for work. That's why Maw beat you. Pity she ain't here now."

Buddy sighed. He put his cup down, pushed his chair away from the table, got up, and began fumbling for pipe and tobacco in the pockets of his disreputable old coat.

"All right, Sarah." He let his voice drop. A moment later he mashed an old hat down on his head and went out the back door. I noticed that his pants had been rolled up at the bottoms because they were too long and his shoes were unlaced.

"He's started in again," my grandmother told me after he wavered past the window, pipe smoke curling around his head. "I got to do something about Joe Ward's drinking."

"What *can* you do?"

"There's ways," she assured me. "Seems like a man that's been through all he has would learn a lesson by the time he's sixty years old."

"I like to hear him tell his dreams," I confessed.

"You just a young boy, Arna, not eleven yet. You wouldn't think they was all that amusing if you'd heard them many times as I have. Joe Ward's been fighting whiskey since he wasn't much older'n you. It's about got the best of him."

A few moments later Buddy was back again, his elbows resting on the window sill as he peered at us through the screen.

"Don't let your grandma turn you against me," he said with a wink.

"You out of your mind, Joe Ward."

"I might be crazy," he argued, "but I got more sense than you have. You don't believe in dreams and you don't believe in ghosts. Anybody knows that's pure crazy. I seen more ghosts than I got fingers and toes. One stopped me on the road the other night."

"Time for you to find something to do now. Get on away

from that window. Go pump some water and fill the trough for the heifers. I noticed it was empty when I was milking this morning. You'll have this boy afraid to leave the house alone—you and your ghosts."

"I wasn't drunk when I seen it neither," he insisted.

"That's *your* opinion. Get busy now."

We heard him singing in a gay, half-falsetto voice as he drew the water and tottered back and forth between the two wooden buckets from the barnyard to the pump. Meanwhile, my grandmother opened the kitchen safe and brought out a fifth of whiskey. Knowing what I did about Buddy, I couldn't help being surprised. Nobody had ever left liquor any place in the house where he could be tempted by it.

"Has that been there all the time?"

"Since day before yesterday," she smiled. "He's seen it too. That's why he's singing so loud. I was looking at him out of the corner of my eye when he helped me set the table this morning. He came across it up there amongst the dishes, and he must of thought Doug forgot and left it when he and Rose were here the other day. Anyhow I saw him pushing it back a little further and trying to hide it so I wouldn't take it away before he could get to it."

My grandmother wasn't given to pranks. She was never cruel, and I wondered why her eyes twinkled as she recalled his sly discovery and the quick-witted maneuver with which he followed it.

"You going to hide it now?"

"No, I'm going to put it back where he can find it—after I fix it."

The "fixing" of which she spoke involved pouring the

whiskey into a bowl and putting several tiny fish in it.

"They say this will turn him against whiskey," she explained confidently.

We stayed in the kitchen the rest of the morning, and Buddy did not return. Several times I saw him come suspiciously near, whistling or singing with a casual air, and throw a quick glance through the screen door or the window. On each occasion he retreated promptly—either toward the front gate or in the direction of the fields behind the barn. Later he moved the grindstone to a position under the willow tree where he could keep an eye on us while working the pedal and grinding the dull blades he found lying about the place.

This pleased my grandmother. Obviously a part of her plan was to keep him waiting, but after a while I went out to watch the fidgety old fellow put new edges on the ax, the garden hoes, the beet knives, and the long scythe. It was a tedious chore, and I knew he was working under a strain.

"Sarah keeps awful busy," he observed, stuffing a handful of tobacco in his cheek.

"She's nearly through," I said.

"That's where you're wrong. You don't know your grandma." His irritation could no longer be concealed. "She'll horse around in that one room all day, sweeping first one way and then the other. She gets on my nerves doing that. I wish she'd go in the front of the house and sit down a while."

She did go soon afterwards, and Buddy touched his moistened thumb against the blade he had been grinding and suddenly discovered that it had a completely satisfactory edge.

"Guess that'll do the business now," he said, stepping gingerly around the grindstone and gathering up the sharpened tools. "Reckon you can hang this scythe in the barn for me?"

I could see through his scheme, but I didn't object.

"I'll take the beet knives too," I said. "I know where they go."

My back was turned, and I had taken a few steps on the path when I heard Buddy muttering behind me.

"Goddamn my unhardlucky soul."

"What's happened?"

He looked flustered when I faced him.

"Nothing—nothing much. Thought I'd cut myself on this old ax, but I guess not."

His real concern, of course, was that Grandma was standing in the screen door again trying hard to hold her mouth straight.

"I s'pose you all don't want no lunch today," she taunted.

Buddy made this the excuse for an explosion.

"Who said so? I work round here all morning and end up by almost cutting the blood out of myself on this devilish ax, and you come talking about no lunch. Goddamit, I'm sick and tired."

"Hush, Joe Ward. Come on in and eat when you get ready. I'll have something waiting."

When I came in to help with the table, I discovered the whiskey in the safe. She had poured it from the bowl back into the bottle, and she had been careful to place it exactly where Buddy had previously hidden it.

Buddy was sullen and dull as he sank into his chair. There was no light behind the cataracts that dimmed his eyes. He had run his hands through his thinning black hair so many times it now looked as it had when he first crawled out of bed in the morning. His mustache had a skimpy, plucked look; his head was bowed; his mouth turned downward.

"I'm going to leave you with it," my grandmother announced suddenly. "Never mind the dishes. I'll do them later."

Buddy perked up a little.

"Where you going?"

"Just out in the front yard. I got a basket of socks to darn. Why don't you come read to me when you get through, Arna?"

I promised I would, and a few moments later I got up and left Buddy with his cold meat and his fantasies. In the living room I stopped at the bookcase and found the copy of *Treasure Island* which we had started. There was a carpet-covered stool in the corner and I took this out too, for there were so many ants you couldn't sit on the ground and read. Grandma was rocking under the pepper tree, the basket of socks beside her, with a lump like an egg bulging from the toe of the one she was working on. When I set the stool directly in front of her, she shook her head.

"Not there. Move it over to the side a little so you can see when he goes out."

"He's leaving now," I noticed.

Buddy was already on the path and headed toward the barn.

"You think it'll cure him, Grandma?"

"They say it will. He won't know anything's wrong with the whiskey. He'll think it's just hisself turning against the taste of the stuff."

It sounded to me like a reasonable idea.

"We tried everything else we knew before we came out here. Sent him down to Keeley's in New Orleans twice. He'd stop drinking for a little while, but not long. After the rest of us came to California, he got so bad he couldn't even hold his job in the bakery. They said he cried like a baby. Promised me faithful he'd never taste another drop if I'd just send for him. Well, I did, and now look at him. Which way did he go?"

"Behind the barn," I said.

"Don't you ever be like him, Arna."

Suddenly a question that intrigued me as much as his drinking popped out, and I found myself asking, "Is that why he never got married and had a family of his own like other men?"

"Well—in a way."

"Didn't he ever act like he wanted to—wasn't there anybody he liked when he was young?"

She slipped the artificial egg out of the sock she was darning and put it in the heel of another. She waited so long to answer I began to think she was going to ignore me. She bit off another strand of yarn.

"No reason why you shouldn't know," she said finally. "Joe Ward went with a girl once. Maw and the rest of us was hoping he'd get married and settle down. He never did."

"Why?"

"They broke up."

She may have been sorry she had opened the subject at all. I have always been a relentless question asker. As far back as I can remember, people have tried to curb my curiosity. Grandma was no exception, but she didn't seem to blame me too much for wanting to know about Buddy. He was fond of me, and I seemed to have more sympathy for him than most others had.

"Well, he's your uncle—your own great uncle, that is—and if I tell you about him, you got to keep it to yourself. Understand?"

"Yes'm, I understand."

"Elvire was a mighty pretty girl," she recalled softly. "Color of a apricot. Hair hanging down her back in two big ropes. Her father was white, of course. Alexandria was full of fine-looking colored people in those days. Elvire was as pretty as Adah Isaacs Menken."

I didn't know who Menken was, but the comparison was impressive as my grandmother pronounced the three names. I could tell she was quoting.

"Who said that, Grandma?"

"Mr. Silas Boatman—he was a business man that came to Alexandria off and on. He'd seen Adah on the stage and off, and he said she'd never known the day when she was any better looking than Elvire Du Plaz. I told him if that was the case then Alexandria had at least a dozen that was Adah's equal in looks. Anyhow, it was this Elvire that Joe Ward started out to keeping company with. That was back —let me see—"

"Before I was born," I supplied.

Grandma smiled.

"Before your mother was born. Let me see, Joe Ward was born during the Rebellion. That would make him about—well, this was in the early eighties. Reconstruction was still on. When him and Elvire danced together at parties, folks gave them plenty room. They was something to see. She had a lot of pretty silk clothes and lace parasols and the like. Joe Ward was a dresser too. Sometimes his hat, his suit, and the strap on his umbrella handle all matched perfect. He could have things like that because he was making good money."

Suddenly I caught a glimpse of Buddy going across the sugar beet fields behind our one-acre plot. The tiny, battered, but still strangely flamboyant old man was nearing the edge of a dark clump beyond.

"There he goes," I interrupted. "He's almost to the swamp."

She didn't even look up from her darning.

"Let him go. Joe Ward always liked to slip off by himself. It was like that when he was a little boy. We'd miss him now and then and find him afterwards back on the shady side of a fence or under a hedge—reading. That's what he liked. You remind me of him sometimes. One thing though: he could spell better'n you. People came from miles around to give him words to spell. He never went to school much either. This was just what Mr. George Kelsey taught him. He learned to be a fancy pastry baker the same way, and he was doing fine by the time him and Elvire started talking about getting married."

"But they never did," I reminded her.

"This Mr. Silas Boatman kept coming around and talking about how Elvire was the prettiest thing he ever saw.

He got so he wanted people to see her. Next he was wondering how she would look in a dress he saw in New Orleans, so he brought it back to her with matching beads and earrings. Then nothing would do but she had to put it on and let some of his friends see her wearing it.

"This went on a good while, but Elvire and Joe Ward didn't stop dancing together. On Sundays they'd row on the river in a boat. Sometimes Joe Ward would get Maw to let him take the horse and buggy, and the two would drive across the river and out around Pineville. They was getting on so nice together it surprised me when he commenced drinking too much. But he had his reasons.

"Once I said something about it—I forget what it was—but he looked at me so sad-like I had to turn my face. So he waited a minute and then said, 'You ask me that, Sarah? *You ask me that question?*' There wasn't nothing left for me to say to him about his drinking after that. It wouldn't have been so bad if another colored man had wanted to marry Elvire and tried to win her away from Joe Ward. Then it would of been just who shall and who sha'n't. But with a right white man like Mr. Boatman, a family man in business down in New Orleans, and things being like they are down home, and the Reconstruction going on and the Klan riding and all, what was a young man like Joe Ward going to do?

"Well, he started doing just what he's doing now—slipping away by hisself with a bottle. He quit seeing Elvire. He quit seeing any women. All he did with his time when he wasn't working was to read magazines and dime novels and drink whiskey. Later he went on to gambling. At his work he behaved peculiar. He made birthday cakes like none you ever heard about. He put funny little decorations on wedding cakes. You could see he didn't know whether to laugh or cry. When Mr. Boatman carried Elvire away to Shreveport and lived with her a while, Joe Ward didn't even hear about it till she was back in town. Nobody would mention it, and he wasn't trying to find out anything.

"Once after that they met. She'd been crying a lot, and folks said she was pretty broken up. Love matches between white and colored were not as popular down home then as they'd been before the Rebellion, and Mr. Boatman couldn't see hisself setting her up in a fine house and all. Some of his friends might criticize him. Maybe they'd started doing it already. On the other hand, there was Joe Ward, acting more like a child than ever in Mr. O'Shea's pastry shop and hiding away with his bottle and his books when he wasn't at work. When she couldn't stand it no longer, Elvire got all dressed up in one of her prettiest silks, put on her best jewelry and a few touches of perfume, and hired a hack to drive her to our house.

"She didn't get out. Instead she sent the driver to call Joe Ward. It was evening. The moon was out, and the leaves of the pecan tree in the yard were just barely moving. When I called Joe Ward, he came out of his room, and I followed him to the front door and stood there and watched him weaving on the path. He wasn't mad with Elvire, so far as I could see. He talked almost like he was glad to see her. 'You look pretty, gal,' he said, 'just as shiny as a star back in the dark there. I'm glad you come by.' That was about as far as he went. She was in favor of letting old things be new again with them—starting over and making up. But by then Joe Ward's liquor had commenced talking, and he wouldn't give her nothing that would make sense. When she started crying and asked the hackman to drive on, he didn't know what to make of it. I was waiting when Joe Ward came back down the path, and I opened the door for him. 'Wonder how come she acted like that?' he asked, child-like. I told him to go on to bed and maybe he'd find out later."

"Did he?" I asked.

"I don't think so," she said.

She rocked a little longer under the tree. Then the breeze from the ocean became cooler, and she suggested that we move inside. This reminded me of the book I hadn't opened yet, and I mentioned it to her.

"Never mind that," she said. "We can read it tonight."

She didn't mention Buddy again that afternoon, and I interested myself in other things. Neither of us expected him to show up for supper, and we were not disappointed. In fact, I think we were both surprised at twilight when we saw him crossing the beet fields with his arms loaded with white flowers. We had gone to the barn to put out some alfalfa and close the chicken coops. It was almost dark enough for a lantern, but it was much too early for Buddy to be getting back from one of his lonely excursions. We walked to the house and waited on the back steps.

Buddy struggled along like a man walking in quicksand. When he reached the yard, we could see the mud still clinging to his clothes. He seemed to be weighted down by it. The masses of white flowers were being crushed in his arms, but they grew more and more vivid in the shadows under the trees. He saw us finally and stood swaying dimly before the steps.

"Well–" Grandma said.

"I'm back, Sarah."

"So I see."

"I found something I thought you and Arna would like."

"You must of found something else too."

"I did," he confessed. "Did you miss it?"

"Was it good?" she asked eagerly.

"Can't you tell?" he asked with a lilt.

"I mean how'd it taste?"

He thought a moment.

"Taste? Don't believe I know. I helt my breath when I drank it. Never did like the *taste* of whiskey."

My grandmother uttered a deep moan. "Put the flowers by the pump," she said. "Go in and get out of them muddy clothes. I don't know what to do with you, Joe Ward."

He seemed ready to cry.

"Don't abuse me, Sarah," he pleaded. "I brought you these flowers."

She took my hand, and I could feel the sternness coming back into her bones as she opened the door.

"Nobody's abusing you, Joe Ward. Do as I say."

"All right, Sarah," he whispered.

He hadn't moved when she closed the door.

TALK TO THE MUSIC

You tells it to the music and
the music tells it to you.
—Sidney Bechet

My father used to say that when you heard one blues song, you've heard them all. He did not mean that all are the same, of course, or that one is enough to satisfy whatever it is in you that craves blues, but after you have listened to one blues, you can always recognize another. In the same way, when you've met one blues singer, you know the species. Ma Rainey, Mayme Smith, Bessie Smith—I could be talking about any one of them and you wouldn't be able to tell by the story which one I had in mind. But right now I'm thinking about the other Mayme—Mayme Dupree.

She never made records, and she never got to Broadway, and nobody ever called her Empress of the Blues, or Lady Day, or anything equivalent, but don't let that fool you. Mayme Dupree had what the others had and then some more. She could play the piano as well as sing and she made up her own songs. You've heard the Jelly-Roll Morton recording of the Mayme Dupree Blues. Well, that's what I'm talking about.

Chances are all this was before your time. What you know about women blues singers probably does not go back any further than Ethel Waters or Pearl Bailey or Billie Holiday, but ask Ethel or Pearl. They'll tell you about Mayme Dupree. Ask Kid Ory or Sidney Bechet. Mayme was singing blues before some of these were born.

There were still other things Mayme had that couldn't be matched by the three more celebrated women who brought the blues out of the South. She was a New Orleans woman with just enough Creole hauteur to make her interesting, and she was good looking. I'm still a bug about old New Orleans—though my own hometown was up the river a piece—and I can't remember a time when I had any objection to good looking women. Naturally I wanted to see and hear this Mayme Dupree people talked about.

But that wasn't easy. Mayme worked as an entertainer, but she worked in Storyville, and that was the legendary red-light district of the fabulous old city at the mouth of the Mississippi. I may have looked young, but age wasn't the obstacle. While there was a good bit of democracy in Storyville, believe me, there was not enough to open the doors of the place where Mayme sang to a black boy who was obviously not one of the employees.

As you know, Jelly-Roll Morton got around this by rushing the can; he made himself available for certain errands. He stood by to run around the corner with the beer can and get it refilled whenever this service was demanded. The wage was negligible, but the job gave the long-legged kid an excuse for being on the premises and provided excellent opportunities for him to hear the aching, heartsick songs of Mayme Dupree.

I, on the other hand, was never any good at masquerades of any kind. They still annoy me. The difference may have been that old Jelly was bent on learning Mayme's songs and nothing else, while I was curious about the singer herself and couldn't stop wondering what it was that troubled her and made her sing the way she did. In any case, I found out where she lived, and the time came when I went there to see her.

I put on my Sunday clothes, which was the only change I had at the time anyhow, fastened my two-toned shoes with a button hook, adjusted the stickpin in my tie, and gave an extra touch to my curly and rather flamboyantly parted hair. I was pleased with the raven sideburns, but my feathers fell when I looked at the mustache. Well, the devil with that, I sighed, but I remained confused as to the kind of impression I wanted to make. As an afterthought, when I had put on my hat and started for the door, I picked up my mandolin case and the leather-covered roll of sheet music beside it.

It was pointless to carry these things everywhere I went, but I had formed the habit, and in almost any new situation I felt more comfortable with them than without. This was especially true in the late afternoon or early evening, and that was the time of day I had chosen to look up Mayme. I felt fine as I strolled on the wooden banquette that still served as a sidewalk in that part of town, but presently my feelings changed to dismay.

Neither the appearance nor the smell of the neighborhood was improving, and the quarters in which I asked for Mayme were over a pool hall. The steps were on the outside and the entrance was dirty; the hall beyond, dark. Here and there a shadow stirred. Something ponderous twisted and turned on a chair and finally spoke.

"You looking for somebody, ha'?"

It was the voice of an old woman, and the odd inflection with which she ended her question was pronounced as if she had started to say *hant* and cut it off in the middle.

"Mayme Dupree," I said.

"Mayme's apt to be sleep. She works at night."

"It's nearly dark now."

"Did you ever try to talk to Mayme when she's just waking up?"

"I don't know her yet, I just want to meet her," I explained.

"Well, you sure picked yourself a time." The old woman got out of the chair with more twisting and straining and started down the hall. "Mayme!" she blasted suddenly. "Mayme, somebody's asking for you here." She pounded the door in passing but continued on, finally disappearing down the hall.

Mayme came out soon afterwards, her lower lip hanging, her eyes almost closed, her hair in a tangle, a dingy garment thrown around her. "Do I know you?" she asked vaguely.

"I expect I've done wrong," I said, stuttering. "You don't know me; I'm from Rapides Parish. I just wanted to talk to you. I aimed to catch you when you were sitting around doing nothing."

"You never catch me sitting around doing nothing," Mayme muttered. "What's your name?"

"Norman Taylor."

Actually she didn't care what my name was. Before I could get the words out, she added, "If I was sitting around, I'd be drinking, I wouldn't be doing nothing."

"I mean I want to hear the blues," I ventured. "I want to hear the blues like you sing them.

Her mind seemed to wander but presently she blurted, "What in the name of God you doing with that thing?"

"Would you like to hear me play something on my mandolin?" I asked.

She shook her head. "Not this early in the evening. I got to get myself together now. I'm not too much on mandolin playing when I'm wide awake."

"I didn't mean to break in on you," I apologized again. "I'll move on now, but can't you tell me when I could hear the blues?"

She yawned, scratching her head with all ten of her fingers. "Come back," she nodded. "Come back again sometime."

I did—about an hour later. She had left her room, but I found her down the block sitting alone in the "family" section of a saloon. There was a bottle of gin on the table, beside it a tiny glass and nothing else. I waited at the door till she noticed me. She gave a shrug which I took to mean 'suit yourself', so I took the seat across the table, and she didn't seem to mind. In fact, she scarcely noticed me again after I sat down.

"Don't you ever talk to anybody?" I asked eventually.

She ignored the question. "I got a hack that picks me up

here every evening. It takes me to—to where I go. I'm waiting for it now."

Suddenly Mayme emptied her glass and put the bottle in her handbag, and I looked up and saw the hack driver standing in the door. He was wearing a frayed Prince Albert and a battered top hat. His shoes were rough, his pants and shirt grimy.

"Well, good-bye," I called.

She turned and smiled rather pleasantly, but she kept on walking, and she didn't actually answer.

A saloon was not a place in which I could feel at ease in those days, but somehow I hesitated to leave. After a few moments I went to the bar in the adjoining section and asked for a glass of beer. I stood there a long time nibbling on the "free lunch" as I drank, and gradually became aware of the activity around me.

The telephone rang frequently. Each time it was answered by the bartender whose name, it seemed, was Benny, and each time the message had to do with someone's need for a musician or a singer or a group to entertain at a party, a dance, a boatride, or some other merry occasion. The men at the bar and those lolling about the premises would prick their ears as soon as Benny took the receiver off the hook, and as quickly as he indicated what kind of performer was sought, one who could fill the bill would step forward. Sometimes the request was for a specific individual or combination, and sometimes those requested were unavailable due to previous engagement. Some were in the pool hall around the corner and had left instructions as to how they might be fetched. A few were independent enough to ask a few questions about the hours, the distance, the pay, and other details before accepting a gig, as they called the engagements, but in the end no job went unfilled, and I was almost tempted to indicate to Benny my own availability.

But I had not come to New Orleans to seek employment as a musician, so I promptly dismissed the idea from my mind. Even though I had already let myself be drawn into several activities which I did not plan to write home about, the temptation to capitalize on my modest musical skills was not strong enough to lure me into another. I had left my parents with the understanding that I would enroll at New Orleans University, and I had every intention of doing so—eventually. My determination to hear the blues first was an irregularity which I considered amply justified. It was not based on mere whim or a casual desire. I had heard strains of the music, and I was haunted. With me the blues had become a strange necessity. I knew that before I could undertake anything else in New Orleans, I had to hear Mayme Dupree sing.

Before leaving that evening, I gained a general impression of the business end of the music game as the boys around New Orleans knew it. While Benny's saloon and Buddy's barber shop, which was mentioned several times during the half hour I stood at the bar, were not employment agencies, they did serve as clearing houses of a sort. There was no competition between the places, and neither expected cuts or payoffs of any kind from the musicians or the employers. Benny was satisfied to have the fellows hang around his place and do their drinking there, and apparently Buddy Bolden's shop was content to shave the musicians and cut their hair. Buddy, of course, was a powerful cornet player and bandman himself, and this made things a little different in his case.

Other women came in after Mayme Dupree left. Some were accompanied by escorts. Others were joined in the "family" section by men who spotted them as they arrived. I did not get the impression that any of these women had come into Benny's to pick up musical gigs. On the contrary, I concluded that most of them were there to be picked up themselves. Like the musicians, they appeared to have slept all day. Getting their eye-openers at Benny's, they looked fresh and sassy, and their perfume filled the saloon. When I turned around and discovered a particularly giddy-looking one trying to trap me with her eyes, I decided it was time for me to look at my watch and go through the motions of hurrying to an appointment.

What Mayme said about the hack picking her up at Benny's every evening was true. She never missed, and the hackman was always on time. I could have set my watch by him. But I did no more than speak and pass the time of day the next few times with her. Mayme did not encourage conversation. Absorbed in her own thoughts, she would come into Benny's saloon just as twilight was falling and go to the most isolated table in the family room. Benny would give her the usual pleasantry as he filled her tiny glass and left the flask of gin beside it, but Mayme's eyes were shadowed by her bird of Paradise hat, and I could see nothing on her face to indicate she even heard him. But I did not give up hope, and the time came when she invited me to come over and have some sit-down.

"You come here pretty regular," she chided.

"You told me to come back sometime," I reminded her.

Mayme smiled. "You're too young a boy to hurrah a woman old as me."

"I couldn't smart-aleck anybody if I wanted to, Mayme," I confessed. "Besides, I've got too much on my mind."

"You still hankering for the blues?"

"I'd give my eye teeth to hear them."

"You look like a boy that's had good raising. You keeps your shoes shined and your hair combed. You ain't got no cause to be hanging around saloons, much less trying to hear boogie house music. If you're a stranger in New Orleans, why don't you try to meet some nice quadroon girls? There's lots of parties going on all the time. Go rowing on Lake Ponchartrain and play your mandolin. That's something you could write home and tell your people about."

"I aim to do all that sometime maybe," I admitted. "But I don't feel like it now. I had a girl at home, pretty as you please, but she couldn't wait. She said I was too slow. I don't want to think about courting or sweet music again for a long, long time. I'd like to hear something lowdown, Mayme."

"I don't sing the blues just to be singing them," she said. "Not any more, I don't. If you want to hear my blues, you got to go where I go, Norman, and I don't rightly think they'd let you in."

"Where's that?"

She put the cork in her bottle. "Storyville," she answered. "Do I have to say any more?"

"The red-light district?"

"That's where I work. That's where this hack is waiting to take me."

The driver was standing in the doorway. She emptied her glass.

"You don't look like a fancy woman, Mayme, and you don't sound much like one."

"Along about nine or ten o'clock I sit down at the piano, and I sets my bottle of gin where I can reach it. I don't stop playing and singing till that bottle's empty. Then I get up and put on my hat. They pay me my money and I go home." She had started toward the door, but since she continued to talk, I followed her out to the hack. Seeing me standing there after she had climbed in, a sudden impulse seemed to strike her. "Get in if you want to," she said. "The hackman will bring you back this way. I don't keep him waiting around down there. He comes back for me in the morning.

Riding beside her in the rented carriage gave me a funny feeling. I had never considered myself a man of the world, but all at once I felt like one. "You ride in style," I told her.

"It takes a big cut out of what I make to pay for it, but it's the only way I can be sure of getting there." She fished in her handbag for cigarets, lit one in the darkness, and settled back for the slow drive. After a long pause she said, half-mischievously, I thought, "If you was out riding with a sure 'nough fancy gal, Norman, it wouldn't be like courting somebody you aimed to marry. You wouldn't study about age or color—things like that—so long as she smelled sweet and was soft to touch."

"If you're not careful, you'll be giving me ideas in a minute," I laughed.

She laughed too, but she added quickly, "Don't pay me no mind, boy. It ain't like me to carry on a lot of foolishness. I don't know what's come over me tonight."

"You're not as unfriendly as you try to make out," I encouraged.

Her answer was something between a sigh and a grunt. "Don't count on it," she added after a pause. "I'm a blue-gummed woman, and I know it. I'm poison, too."

"Aw, hush, Mayme."

"Don't hush me. I know what I'm saying. I bit a man once. It was just a love bite, but his arm swelled up like he'd been bit by a black widow spider or a copperhead snake."

"I don't pay any attention to the foolishness I hear people talk about blue-gummed women, women with crooked eyes, right black women. I'd go out with a girl that was black as a new buggy if I liked her, and I think blue gums are kind of interesting."

"Just go on thinking that," she scoffed, "and one of these days you'll find yourself all swoll up like a man with the dropsy."

The lights were coming on in Storyville as we reached the district, and there was a good bit of going and coming in the streets. Saloons were hitting it up, and in some the tinkle of glasses dissolved into a background of ragtime piano thumping. But the over-all mood, as I sensed it, was grim, and furtive shadows moved along the street. Can desire be anything but sad? I wondered as the carriage pulled up beside an ornate hitching post. I jumped out and waited for Mayme to put her foot on a large square-cut steppingstone.

"Is this as far as I can go?" I asked, looking up at the elegant doorway at the top of the steps.

"Here is where you turn back," she said.

"If there's any way you can fix it for me to hear you sing sometime," I reminded her, "I'll sure appreciate it, Mayme."

She didn't promise, but her voice still sounded indulgent as she let the hackman go, instructing him to drop me at a convenient point in the vicinity of Benny's.

I had enough mother wit to realize that Mayme was not the kind of woman you could persuade to do anything before she was good and ready. Having made it clear to her what I wanted, I settled back to another long wait, taking pains to let her see me occasionally and making sure she got a good chance to say anything that happened to be on her mind. Meanwhile, Benny's saloon hummed nightly. The telephone rang. Musicians were in and out, whistling for hacks, catching quick drinks before hurrying off to their gigs. Fancy women as bright as flamingos fluttered in and settled down languidly at the family tables And the giddy-looking one who had taken a shine to me kept making eyes.

Mayme's hack driver had appeared in the saloon and she had followed him out one evening when the place was more crowded than usual, but a few moments later he returned and tapped me on the shoulder.

"She wants to speak to you," he said.

I didn't wait to finish my sweeten' water (gin and rock candy), and when I reached the carriage, Mayme was leaning out with something to tell me. "They need a boy tonight—out at the place. Did you ever work in a white coat?"

"Does it matter?" I asked, climbing in beside her. "I'll wear one tonight and like it."

"Well, just mind your p's and q's. Keep a duster or a broom or a towel in your hand all the time and don't sit down. Somebody might ask you to do something every now and then, but if you don't pay them no mind, they won't pay you none. Anybody looks at you right hard, just kind of ease around and go to dusting the woodwork or picking up empty glasses."

That was as much as I needed, and when Mayme presented me to the Madame as a boy who could take the place of some vague Leroy whom they did not expect to show up, we both nodded without speaking. She was a large woman, heavily jewelled, with glossy black hair piled on her head in great rolls. Her accent was French, but I couldn't be sure whether she was a Louisiana quadroon or a woman from southern Europe. It didn't matter. She led me out to the back and pointed to Leroy's closet. The equipment was in line with Mayme's description of the job: freshly starched white coat, a hanger for the one I was wearing, towels, lamp rags, dust cloths, mops, brushes, and the rest.

I put on the white coat and crept obsequiously into the big living room. When Mayme began playing the piano, I retreated into a corner where there were several pieces of erotic sculpture which I suddenly decided needed dusting. I think I succeeded in fading into the furniture and the fixtures, because neither the men who came through the front door nor the girls who glided down the stairs gave me a second glance. Presently Mayme took their minds completely away.

> *Good morning, blues,*
> *Heard you when you opened my door.*
> *I said, good morning, blues.*
> *I heard you when you opened my door.*

The sadness of the blues stabbed me with her first line, and immediately I wanted to ask Mayme Dupree who had hurt her and how and what made her take it so hard. Remembering how long she had kept me waiting to hear this first song and the price I'd had to pay—putting off my enrollment in college, hanging around Benny's, and now coming to this place with a dust cloth in my hand—I doubted that I could ever expect to learn what it was that made her sing as she did.

Men were calling for drinks and gals before she finished "Good-morning, Blues." The heavy beat of Mayme's song started things moving. When it was over, she reached for her bottle with one hand while the other hand kept up the rhythm. Then for a long spell the piano carried it alone, but more than once I was sure I saw Mayme press her lips together tightly as she played, like somebody deeply troubled in mind. Eventually she blurted another song as if she could hold it back no longer.

> *If I could holler like the mountain jack,*
> *If I could holler like the mountain jack,*
> *I'd go up on the mountain and call my lover back.*

This was heady stuff, even for the hard-bitten habitués of Storyville, and the way Mayme sang it promptly went to the heads of some. One of the men responded with a sort of hog-calling yell that was not intended as a joke and did not provoke laughter. A girl closed her eyes and fluttered her hands high in the air. A few couples stood together as if to dance but did not move. I began wondering when Mayme would sing the song for which she was becoming known and which I had heard about all the way up in Rapides Parish.

Finally she got around to it—the blues that she had made up herself and that had started a sort of craze among the few people who had been fortunate enough to hear her sing it.

Two-nineteen done took my baby away
Two-nineteen done took my baby away
Two-seventeen bring him back someday.

Everyone seemed to expect her to repeat it several times, adding new verses as she sang, and she kept on until she could somehow get the folks to take their eyes off her and think about themselves again. But all I could think as I listened to Mayme Dupree sing her blues that night was that the blues are sad, terribly sad, and desire is sad too. The bottle of gin on the piano, the erotic sculpture, the motionless dancers, the girls with the flutters, the hog-calling man—all seemed to go very well with Mayme's blues. But I wondered if she thought so.

When I asked her, after I had been back several times, she did not show much interest. The blues she sang were just blues to her. There was nothing special about them. They were neither good nor bad. She could understand how some people might like them but not how anyone would want to talk about them. But I thought I would be ungrateful if I didn't make some effort to tell her how I felt about her songs.

I was convinced that there was power of some kind in the blues, their rhythms, and their themes. Fallen angels could never have wailed like this, no matter how they grieved over paradise. Adam and Eve might have perhaps, crying over their lost innocence, but somehow song was not given to them.

She pondered this conceit as the hack jogged homeward in the early dawn, and I thought it was making a good impression until she suddenly said, "You're crazy."

LONESOME BOY, SILVER TRUMPET

When Bubber first learned to play the trumpet, his old grandpa winked his eye and laughed.

"You better mind how you blow that horn, sonny boy. You better mind."

"I like to blow loud, I like to blow fast, and I like to blow high," Bubber answered. "Listen to this, Grandpa." And he went on blowing with his eyes closed.

When Bubber was a little bigger, he began carrying his trumpet around with him wherever he went, so his old grandpa scratched his whiskers, took the corncob pipe out of his mouth, and laughed again.

"You better mind *where* you blow that horn, boy," he warned. "I used to blow one myself, and I know."

Bubber smiled. "Where did you ever blow music, Grandpa?"

"Down in New Orleans and all up and down the river. I blowed trumpet most everywhere in my young days, and

I tell you, you better mind where you go blowing."

"I like to blow my trumpet in the school band when it marches, I like to blow it on the landing when the river-boats come in sight, and I like to blow it among the trees in the swamp," he said, still smiling. But when he looked at his grandpa again, he saw a worried look on the old man's face, and he asked, "What's the matter, Grandpa, ain't that all right?"

Grandpa shook his head. "I wouldn't do it if I was you."

That sounded funny to Bubber, but he was not in the habit of disputing his grandfather. Instead he said, "I don't believe I ever heard you blow the trumpet, Grandpa. Don't you want to try blowing on mine now?"

Again the old man shook his head. "My blowing days are long gone," he said. "I still got the lip, but I ain't got the teeth. It takes good teeth to blow high notes on a horn, and these I got ain't much good. They're store teeth."

That made Bubber feel sorry for his grandfather, so he whispered softly, "I'll mind where I blow my horn, Grandpa."

He didn't really mean it though. He just said it to make his grandpa feel good. And the very next day he was half a mile out in the country blowing his horn in a cornfield. Two or three evenings later he was blowing it on a shady lane when the sun went down and not paying much attention where he went.

When he came home, his grandpa met him. "I heard you blowing your horn a long ways away," he said. "The air was still. I could hear it easy."

"How did it sound, Grandpa?"

"Oh, it sounded right pretty." He paused a moment, knocking the ashes out of his pipe, before adding, "Sounded like you mighta been lost."

That made Bubber ashamed of himself, because he knew he had not kept his word and that he was not minding where he blowed his trumpet. "I know what you mean, Grandpa," he answered. "But I can't do like you say. When I'm blowing my horn, I don't always look where I'm going."

Grandpa walked to the window and looked out. While he was standing there, he hitched his overalls up a little higher. He took a red handkerchief from his pocket and wiped his forehead. "Sounded to me like you might have been past Barbin's Landing."

"I was lost," Bubber admitted.

"You can end up in some funny places when you're just blowing a horn and not paying attention. I know," Grandpa insisted. "I know."

"Well, what do you want me to do, Grandpa?"

The old man struck a kitchen match on the seat of his pants and lit a kerosene lamp because the room was black dark by now. While the match was still burning, he lit his pipe. Then he sat down and stretched out his feet. Bubber was on a stool on the other side of the room, his trumpet under his arm. "When you go to school and play your horn in the band, that's all right," the old man said. "When you come home, you ought to put it in the case and leave it there. It ain't good to go trapesing around with a horn in your hand. You might get into devilment."

"But I feel lonesome without my trumpet, Grandpa,"

Bubber pleaded. "I don't like to go around without it any-time. I feel lost."

Grandpa sighed. "Well, there you are—lost with it and lost without it. I don't know what's going to become of you, sonny boy."

"You don't understand, Grandpa. You don't under-stand."

The old man smoked his pipe quietly for a few minutes and then went off to bed, but Bubber did not move. Later on, however, when he heard his grandpa snoring in the next room, he went outdoors, down the path, and around the smokehouse, and sat on a log. The night was still. He couldn't hear anything louder than a cricket. Soon he be-gan wondering how his trumpet would sound on such a still night, back there behind the old smokehouse, so he put the mouthpiece to his lips very lightly and blew a few silvery notes. Immediately Bubber felt better. Now he knew for sure that Grandpa didn't understand how it was with a boy and a horn—a lonesome boy with a silver trum-pet. Bubber lifted his horn toward the stars and let the music pour out.

Presently a big orange moon rose, and everything Bub-ber could see changed suddenly. The moon was so big it made the smokehouse and the trees and the fences seem small. Bubber blew his trumpet loud, he blew it fast, and he blew it high, and in just a few minutes he forgot all about Grandpa sleeping in the house.

He was afraid to talk to Grandpa after that. He was afraid Grandpa might scold him or warn him or try in some other way to persuade him to leave his trumpet in its case. Bubber was growing fast now. He knew what he liked, and he did not think he needed any advice from Grandpa.

Still he loved his grandfather very much, and he had no intention of saying anything that would hurt him. Instead he decided to leave home. He did not tell Grandpa what he was going to do. He just waited till the old man went to sleep in his bed one night. Then he quietly blew out the lamp, put his trumpet under his arm, and started walking down the road from Marksville to Barbin's Landing.

No boat was there, but Bubber did not mind. He knew one would come by before morning, and he knew that he wouldn't be lonesome so long as he had his trumpet with him. He found a place on the little dock where he could lean back against a post and swing his feet over the edge while playing, and the time passed swiftly And when he finally went aboard a riverboat, just before morning, he found a place on the deck that suited him just as well and went right on blowing his horn.

Nobody asked him to pay any fare. The riverboat men did not seem to expect it of a boy who blew a trumpet the way Bubber did. And in New Orleans the cooks in the kitchens where he ate and the people who kept the rooming houses where he slept did not seem to expect him to pay either. In fact, people seemed to think that a boy who played a trumpet where the patrons of a restaurant could hear him or for the guests of a rooming house should receive money for it. They began to throw money around Bubber's feet as he played his horn.

At first he was surprised. Later he decided it only

showed how wrong Grandpa had been about horn blowing. So he picked up all the money they threw, bought himself fancy new clothes, and began looking for new places to play. He ran into boys who played guitars or bullfiddles or drums or other instruments, and he played right along with them. He went out with them to play for picnics or barbecues or boat excursions or dances. He played early in the morning and he played late at night, and he bought new clothes and dressed up so fine he scarcely knew himself in a mirror. He scarcely knew day from night.

It was wonderful to play the trumpet like that, Bubber thought, and to make all that money. People telephoned to the rooming house where he lived and asked for him nearly every day. Some sent notes asking if he would play his trumpet at their parties. Occasionally one would send an automobile to bring him to the place, and this was the best of all. Bubber liked riding through the pretty part of the city to the ballrooms in which well-dressed people waited to dance to his music. He enjoyed even more the times when he was taken to big white-columned houses in the country, houses surrounded by old trees with moss on them.

But he went to so many places to play his trumpet, he forgot where he had been and he got into the habit of not paying much attention. That was how it was the day he received a strange call on the telephone. A voice that sounded like a very proper gentleman said, "I would like to speak to the boy from Marksville, the one who plays the trumpet."

"I'm Bubber, sir. I'm the one."

"Well, Bubber, I'm having a very special party tonight —very special," the voice said. "I want you to play for us."

Bubber felt a little drowsy because he had been sleeping when the phone rang, and he still wasn't too wide awake. He yawned as he answered, "Just me, sir? You want me to play by myself?"

"There will be other musicians, Bubber. You'll play in the band. We'll be looking for you?"

"Where do you live, sir?" Bubber asked sleepily.

"Never mind about that, Bubber. I'll send my chauffeur with my car. He'll bring you."

The voice was growing faint by this time, and Bubber was not sure he caught the last words. "Where did you say, sir?" he asked suddenly. "When is it you want me?"

"I'll send my chauffeur," the voice repeated and then faded out completely.

Bubber put the phone down and went back to his bed to sleep some more. He had played his trumpet very late the night before, and now he just couldn't keep his eyes open.

Something was ringing when he woke up again. Was it the telephone? Bubber jumped out of bed and ran to answer, but the phone buzzed when he put it to his ear. There was nobody on the line. Then he knew it must have been the doorbell. A moment later he heard the door open, and footsteps came down the dark hall toward Bubber's room. Before Bubber could turn on the light, the footsteps were just outside his room, and a man's voice said, "I'm the chauffeur. I've brought the car to take you to the dance."

"So soon?" Bubber asked, surprised.

The man laughed. "You must have slept all day. It's night now, and we have a long way to drive."

"I'll put on my clothes," Bubber said.

The street light was shining through the window, so he did not bother to switch on the light in his room. Bubber never liked to open his eyes with a bright light shining, and anyway he knew right where to put his hands on the clothes he needed. As he began slipping into them, the chauffeur turned away. "I'll wait for you on the curb," he said.

"All right," Bubber called. "I'll hurry."

When he finished dressing, Bubber took his trumpet off the shelf, closed the door of his room, and went out to where the tall driver was standing beside a long, shiny automobile. The chauffeur saw him coming and opened the door to the back seat. When Bubber stepped in, he threw a lap robe across his knees and closed it. Then the chauffeur went around to his place in the front seat, stepped on the starter, switched on his headlights, and sped away.

The car was finer than any Bubber had ridden in before; the motor purred so softly and the chauffeur drove it so smoothly, that Bubber soon began to feel sleepy again. One thing puzzled him, however. He had not yet seen the driver's face, and he wondered what the man looked like. But now the chauffeur's cap was down so far over his eyes and his coat collar was turned up so high Bubber could not see his face at all, no matter how far he leaned forward.

After a while he decided it was no use. He would have

to wait till he got out of the car to look at the man's face. In the meantime he would sleep. Bubber pulled the lap robe up over his shoulders, stretched out on the wide back seat of the car and went to sleep again.

The car came to a stop, but Bubber did not wake up till the chauffeur opened the door and touched his shoulder. When he stepped out of the car, he could see nothing but dark, twisted trees with moss hanging from them. It was a dark and lonely place, and Bubber was so surprised he did not remember to look at the chauffeur's face. Instead, he followed the tall figure up a path covered with leaves to a white-columned house with lights shining in the windows.

Bubber felt a little better when he saw the big house with the bright windows. He had played in such houses before, and he was glad for a chance to play in another. He took his trumpet from under his arm, put the mouthpiece to his lips, and blew a few bright, clear notes as he walked. The chauffeur did not turn around. He led Bubber to a side entrance, opened the door, and pointed the boy to the room where the dancing had already started. Without ever showing his face, the chauffeur closed the door and returned to the car.

Nobody had to tell Bubber what to do now. He found a place next to the big fiddle that made the rhythms, waited a moment for the beat, then came in with his trumpet. With the bass fiddle, the drums, and the other stringed instruments backing him up, Bubber began to bear down on his trumpet. This was just what he liked. He played loud, he played fast, he played high, and it was all he could do to keep from laughing when he thought about Grandpa and remembered how the old man had told him to mind how he played his horn. Grandpa should see him now, Bubber thought.

Bubber looked at the dancers swirling on the ballroom floor under the high swinging chandelier, and he wished that Grandpa could somehow be at the window and see how they glided and spun around to the music of his horn. He wished the old man could get at least one glimpe of the handsome dancers, the beautiful women in bright-colored silks, the slender men in black evening clothes.

As the evening went on, more people came and began dancing. The floor became more and more crowded, and Bubber played louder and louder, faster and faster, and by midnight the gay ballroom seemed to be spinning like a pinwheel. The floor looked like glass under the dancers' feet. The drapes on the windows resembled gold, and Bubber was playing his trumpet so hard and so fast his eyes looked like they were ready to pop out of his head.

But he was not tired. He felt as if he could go on playing like this forever. He did not even need a short rest. When the other musicians called for a break and went outside to catch a breath of fresh air, he kept right on blowing his horn, running up the scale and down, hitting high C's, swelling out on the notes and then letting them fade away. He kept the dancers entertained till the full band came back, and he blew the notes that started them to dancing again.

Bubber gave no thought to the time, and when a breeze began blowing through the tall windows, he paid no attention. He played as loud as ever, and the dancers swirled just as fast. But there was one thing that did bother him a little. The faces of the dancers began to look thin and hollow as the breeze brought streaks of morning mist into the room. What was the matter with them? Were they tired from dancing all night? Bubber wondered.

But the morning breeze blew stronger and stronger. The curtains flapped, and a gray light appeared in the windows. By this time Bubber noticed that the people who were dancing had no faces at all, and though they continued to dance wildly as he played his trumpet, they seemed dim and far away. Were they disappearing?

Soon Bubber could scarcely see them at all. Suddenly he wondered where the party had gone. The musicians too grew dim and finally disappeared. Even the room with the big chandelier and the golden drapes on the windows was fading away like a technicolor dream. Bubber was frightened when he realized that nothing was left, and he was alone. Yes, definitely, he was alone—but *where?* Where was he now?

He never stopped blowing his shiny trumpet. In fact, as the party began to break up in this strange way, he blew harder than ever to help himself feel brave again. He also closed his eyes. That was why he happened to notice how uncomfortable the place where he was sitting had become. It was about as unpleasant as sitting on a log. And it was while his eyes were closed that he first became aware of leaves nearby, leaves rustling and blowing in the cool breeze.

But he could not keep his eyes closed for long with so much happening. Bubber just had to peep eventually, and when he did, he saw only leaves around him. Certainly leaves were nothing to be afraid of, he thought, but it was a little hard to understand how the house and room in which he had been playing for the party all night had been replaced by branches and leaves like this. Bubber opened both his eyes wide, stopped blowing his horn for a moment, and took a good, careful look at his surroundings.

Only then did he discover for sure that he was not in a house at all. There were no dancers, no musicians, nobody at all with him, and what had seemed like a rather uncomfortable chair or log was a large branch. Bubber was sitting in a pecan tree, and now he realized that this was where he had been blowing his trumpet so fast and so loud and so high all night. It was very discouraging.

But where was the chauffeur who had brought him here and what had become of the party and the graceful dancers? Bubber climbed down and began looking around. He could see no trace of the things that had seemed so real last night, so he decided he had better go home. Not home to the rooming house where he slept while in New Orleans, but home to the country where Grandpa lived.

He carried his horn under his arm, but he did not play a note on the bus that took him back to Marksville next day. And when he got off the bus and started walking down the road to Grandpa's house in the country, he still didn't feel much like playing anything on his trumpet.

Grandpa was sleeping in a hammock under a chinaberry tree when he arrived, but he slept with one eye open, so Bubber did not have to wake him up. He just stood there, and Grandpa smiled.

"I looked for you to come home before now," the old man said.

"I should have come home sooner," Bubber answered, shamefaced.

"I expected you to be blowing on your horn when you came."

"That's what I want to talk to you about, Grandpa."

The old man sat up in the hammock and put his feet on the ground. He scratched his head and reached for his hat. "Don't tell me anything startling," he said. "I just woke up, and I don't want to be surprised so soon."

Bubber thought maybe he should not mention what had happened. "All right, Grandpa," he whispered, looking rather sad. He leaned against the chinaberry tree, holding the trumpet under his arm, and waited for Grandpa to speak again.

Suddenly the old man blinked his eyes as if remembering something he had almost forgotten. "Did you mind how you blew on that horn down in New Orleans?" he asked.

"Sometimes I did. Sometimes I *didn't*," Bubber confessed.

Grandpa looked hurt. "I hate to hear that, sonny boy," he said. "Have you been playing your horn at barbecues and boat rides and dances and all such as that?"

"Yes, Grandpa," Bubber said, looking at the ground.

"Keep on like that and you're apt to wind up playing for a devil's ball."

Bubber nodded sadly. "Yes, I know."

Suddenly the old man stood up and put his hand on

Bubber's shoulder. "Did a educated gentleman call you on the telephone?"

"He talked so proper I could hardly make out what he was saying."

"Did the chauffeur come in a long shiny car?"

Bubber nodded again. "I ended up in a pecan tree," he told Grandpa.

"I tried to tell you, Bubber, but you wouldn't listen to me."

"I'll listen to you from now on, Grandpa."

Grandpa laughed through his whiskers. "Well, take your trumpet in the house and put it on the shelf while I get you something to eat," he said.

Bubber smiled too. He was hungry, and he had not tasted any of Grandpa's cooking for a long time.

A WOMAN
WITH A MISSION

The circumstances under which Mrs. Eulalie Rainwater discovered the strange genius were almost incredible.

"Fancy," she exclaimed, languishing upon a heap of rich cushions in her sun parlor. "Just fancy, darling. It's the most astonishing thing that ever happened to me. Positively overwhelming. Take these dishes away, Lottie, I can't eat another bite. Excitement at my age—"

Lottie, the brown girl, nodded and reached for the tea things. As a maid her position was distinctly exceptional in Mrs. Rainwater's Larchmont home. For Lottie herself was somewhat of a discovery too where the wealthy old woman was concerned, though indeed a minor one. A little thing always leads to a bigger one, however; and since Lottie represented the starting point of Mrs. Rainwater's artistic interest in Negroes, her value could not be overestimated now that the genius was in hand.

"Have a cigaret?"

"Yes, please." The girl stood before her with the tray.

"He has a finer voice than Roland Hayes, and he's as charming and unspoiled as Robeson. But he must be brought along very carefully. The wrong influences might ruin everything."

"He'll have temptations," Lottie agreed discreetly. "There'll be opportunities to sing in Harlem night clubs and possibly with revues like the *Blackbirds*."

"He mustn't think of it," Mrs. Rainwater said emphatically. "To prostitute a voice like Leander Holly's would be a ringing crime. It would wreck all my plans for him at one stroke. I couldn't allow it under any conditions."

Lottie went into the kitchen. Somehow she could not help feeling glad with Mrs. Rainwater—glad and tremulous at once, in fact; for Lottie knew even better than the old white-haired woman what unhappy possibilities lay ahead of the young singer. But Mrs. Rainwater was so sweet, so good, so perfect in her relations to the young people she "encouraged" that the girl was not able to entertain a genuine foreboding. The little fairy world that revolved around that tender old goddess was not real anyhow, Lottie thought; one could never be convinced that it was not a dream. Naturally, earthly hazards and earthly dangers couldn't enter. It was as safe as any other make-believe place.

At first Mrs. Rainwater's love had run to American Indians. She estimated that she had helped nearly a thousand artists and students who showed her projects involving this romantic group. As a result of her encouragement and her investments, she could point to several creditable books of folk lore, a distinguished body of paintings, a bit of fiction and music, and scores of scholarly works dealing with skull measurements and the like. Most of the latter had never been published, being of doubtful interest to the larger reading public, but Mrs. Rainwater preserved each one in a fire-proof vault. Now in her declining years, partly because of ennui and partly because the former field was nearly exhausted, she had turned to the Negro.

It was odd that she had not considered him earlier, yet she could well account for the tardy recognition. Her interest in the more primitive American groups was not an ordinary interest. Mrs. Rainwater had a philosophy: she was a woman with a mission. It was in her bosom like a patriotic duty, like a religion.

The refined races have lost something vital, an essential vitamin, a certain mystic power. Fortunately for America (and for her theory) this touch was still to be found in the United States. The Navajos had it moderately, but the Negroes possessed it in abundance. Her search for it was like isolating a difficult microbe. This much was difinite: the thing was most evident in artistic expression. There were strange lost currents that these people touched when they sang, when they wrote poetry, even when they told stories.

"It is a precious heritage, a treasure from the jungle," she explained. "We must get our hands on it at any cost."

"Funny," Lottie always said. "Funny I never thought of that."

"Why, of course you didn't, you poor dear. Just another child playing with diamonds."

Mrs. Rainwater did not make the mistake of revealing all that was in her mind. Even to Lottie she did not tell everything. Her plans were her own. The girl was several times tempted to ask, "Well what are you going to have us do with this spiritual gift when we've pinned it down?" But the old woman easily read her thoughts.

"I have important designs for you youngsters, but you mustn't ask me what they are now. Just let us hold everything in strict confidence. No strangers must enter our circle, Lottie. You must help me explain it to Leander. It is such a private matter, so delicate and yet so weighty, that I tremble to think how I'll convey all its implications to that extraordinary young man."

"I think he'll understand," the girl remarked.

The frail gray woman sat for hours on her sun porch. Stacks of the newest books were nearby, but she seldom touched them now. She felt as crisp and insecure as a dry leaf on a bough. Leander Holly's genius filled her sky with big contending winds. She was arranging for his future voice training; she was definitely making it possible for him to live without economic distress. That much was accomplished. But how could she safeguard him from dangerous Harlem influences, from the Tisdale crowd, for example?

Well, one thing that would help was to have him move across to Jersey. There he'd be safe from the night life. He would have time to practice and an opportunity to see the green earth occasionally. And that degraded dilettante, Tisdale (the opprobrium was her own), would be less likely to ensnare the youth. Mrs. Rainwater reached for a sheet of linen note paper. She would engineer that move at once.

* * *

The discovery was now nearly a year in the past, but it remained as vivid as yesterday. It had been such a masterpiece of detection. Mrs. Rainwater never liked to have a genius presented to her; she never liked to have one seek her or make an appeal. She distrusted all such comers. A curious instinct told her that valuable gems are to be found only in unexpected places.

Naturally her heart thumped and her breath came short when, following a red cap through the Grand Central station and down the platform to her train, she suddenly heard a silvery voice singing *Du Bist Du Ruh.* A Negro tenor was singing the German words.

"Oh." The old woman trembled. Her doll-blue eyes turned to heaven, like the eyes of an ancient prophetess. She might have expected to see white doves circling overhead, but the singing was quite enough. She put one hand to her breast and again uttered that throbbing little word, "Oh."

Leander paused with the leather bags as if waiting for her to catch up. Actually he was wondering if she heard his song through the hum of the crowd, wondering if he had modulated the tone so as to sound innocent and unintentional and yet still managed to be heard.

"What number did you say your seat was, ma'am?"

"Oh." Her thoughts were far away. Then, with excitement, "Yes, yes. Here is my ticket. See?"

"Thank you."

"And what is *your* number?"

He pointed to his button.

In her seat she managed to say, "Do you like German songs?"

"Quite well," he said. "Next to spirituals."

He was small for a red cap, slight and brown and clean. His manners were easy and gracious, and Mrs. Rainwater would have asked a few more questions, but the train was leaving.

"I know your chief," she said. "Ezra High. The chief of the red caps. Will you tell him Mrs. Rainwater said to telephone her tonight?"

"I surely will."

He began singing again as he walked through the train. It was a little self-conscious, a trifle showy, but Mrs. Rainwater understood. Primitive. Unspoiled. She was certain that he did not *feel* self-conscious, that he did not mean to be ostentatious. And of course he knew nothing of her. It would be absurd to think that the poor boy was seeking to attract a patron under circumstances like this. Mrs. Rainwater convinced herself on that point and settled back into the seat with folded hands and set purpose.

The boy swung off the train just as it got in motion and hurried up to the red caps' locker room. Inside the door he slapped his palms together, sailed his cap across the room, and cut a few brief pigeon wings. Something like an imprisoned bird quaked and fluttered in his breast.

Ezra High, an old West Indian mulatto, watched him with amused eyes.

"Did you see her?" he asked.

"See her!" The boy was beside himself. "Everything is peaches. She heard me and asked my number. Then she told me to have you call her tonight."

"She'll see you through if she takes a fancy to you," the chief said. "That's all she's been doing for thirty years.

I worked for her husband. He owned the Rainwater Line—coast steamers. And I mean he left her plenty. She's sponsored hundreds of young college folks. This Negro fever is something new, though. She must have read that book called *The New Negro*."

"Lordy, it ain't true," Leander said. "It must be a mistake. You don't mean she might see me through the conservatory—music lessons and all that?"

"She always allowed the others about two hundred a month outside of extras, trips, presents, and whatnot."

Leander put his hand on the old fellow's shoulder.

"I can't tote no more leather today, chief. I got castles to build."

That night the plot was completed, and the next evening Leander went to Larchmont to sing for Mrs. Rainwater. The old woman sat rapt throughout a performance in which the boy sang about a dozen songs accompanied by Lottie. While he was doing a group of spirituals, she wept softly. Her eyes, so blue and moist they suggested the eyes of a baby, turned to the ceiling again and again. Mrs. Rainwater's heart was too full; it was overflowing.

Lottie made cocktails, and the three drank in silence. A little later the old woman drew Leander aside.

"You have a rare gift," she said faintly. "A very rare gift."

"Thank you."

There was a pause.

"Are you getting the best possible training?"

"The best I can afford," he told her.

"Yes, yes. Of course you are, poor boy. Well I have something to suggest for your development, but I'd rather put it in a note. I'll write you a letter tomorrow. Your people have something precious, a spiritual heritage from the jungle that informs your art with a quality that America needs. It would be a calamity to have it lost, wasted."

She was almost whispering the words. It was told as if it were the revelation of a secret. Leander was entranced. He glanced at luxury around him and knew beyond doubt that he had been ushered into a dream world.

He returned to Harlem with Lottie and spent half the night discussing the amazing old woman with the girl who had been her maid for several years. He learned what Mrs. Rainwater gave and what she *expected*. There was an unwritten code to which all her young geniuses were required to subscribe. There was her theory about spiritual currents among primitive people; he would have to respect that. There was the odd obsession she had for writing letters. She generally sent one a day—in her own hand—to the people she happened to be sponsoring at the moment, and she always expected a good, fond answer. She never trusted conversation. To be authentic the entire discourse had to be repeated in the calm meditation of a personal letter. Then there was the matter of secrecy. Leander would be under oath to hold in confidence all Mrs. Rainwater's words, her gifts. She always spoke of those who told as traitors. She was forever admonishing them not to betray her.

These last words seemed rather strong to Leander. He could not understand why she should be so sharp in upbraiding the overjoyed young people who only recounted her goodness and generosity, but he was willing to conform, no matter what the restrictions. Still he did find it hard to imagine the gentle old woman in a huff.

The boy sang boldly as he walked up Edgecombe Avenue to the row of apartment houses on the hill. A milkman's wagon rumbled in the quiet street.

The move to Jersey did not displease Leander. It was indeed a small concession to make in return for the large gifts he had received. Coming thus at the end of a year's patronage and explained in a small, solemn note, the request seemed utterly reasonable. So while he found the little cities of Jersey dreary as compared to Harlem, he was able to convince himself that Mrs. Rainwater's decision was made in his interest. He settled down in Montclair and devoted his time to vocal exercises and daily letters to what he soon began to call (in his mind) the "throne."

This last chore was at first like punching a time clock, and more disagreeable. The letters Mrs. Rainwater expected constituted a sort of spiritual diary, something like a confessional. Leander found that the ones she enjoyed most were those in which he praised her mystic insight and told her how her wisdom had filled his life with meaning by revealing the great unnoticed forces that stirred his soul. She would take no thanks for her financial aid, but she could not hear enough of this other praise. And Leander developed a formula that made writing reasonably easy after the first six months.

Mrs. Rainwater decided that to be consistent with her treatment of geniuses Lottie should move to Montclair also. Lottie had storytelling gifts. She would probably never make a writer of consequence but she could collect bright sayings of Negroes. That would make a worthy project. Her list might grow so long that it could be indexed and become a reference compendium. Bright sayings of Negroes—the idea was fascinating. Lottie might be given more leisure for this work, and Montclair was just the place for her. There she could be an asset to Leander, playing accompaniments for him and helping to keep him away from Harlem's lights.

For this the boy was genuinely thankful. Lottie's room was just around the corner and he found her good company. And he soon learned to his complete astonishment and delight that the girl was as ready for a let up as he was. They were just a pair of wooly-headed urchins straying on celestial streets. Each had been homeless and nearly destitute before the good angel found them, and each looked upon himself as a clever imposter in the role of genius. They laughed at the studied guile by which they maintained their positions. After all, they were just ordinary young people. Their talents—well, they wouldn't fuss with her about that.

"Whenever I want a present," Lottie said, "I give her one first. Like last week. I'd been hinting how I needed a fur coat. I made sure she had it well in mind; then I let it drop for a few days. All of a sudden I lit on the right medicine. I found a phonograph record of the African Zulu singers that toured England. I paid a dollar for it and had it sent by mail. Two days later the fur coat came. She likes to have you make her little 'artistic' presents. That gives her an excuse to lay out the cash on you."

"Thanks," Leander laughed. "I need a good Gladstone bag. I'll send her that little voodoo drum I have."

"It's just the thing, but you don't have to stop at a Gladstone bag. You can just as easily get a wardrobe trunk and an overcoat in the bargain."

That night the two left their cages and ran over to Harlem for a few dances at the Savoy. Afterwards they went to an odd little place where there was food and drink and the entertainment was informal. The manager, an old friend, asked for a song and Leander obliged with a popular number. When he had finished, a handsome white-haired man invited the singer to meet some downtown visitors. At his own table again, Leander introduced the man to Lottie.

"Mr. Tisdale—"

"How do you do."

When he was gone, Lottie touched Leander's knee.

"That's the one," she whispered. "He's the one Mrs. Rainwater calls the 'degraded dillitante.' They're old enemies."

"Yes? I liked him," Leander said.

"Don't tell her that. Lordy, she'd die."

"That's foolish."

"Foolish I know, but it's gospel. They're both interested in Negroes, but they got different ways of showing it. He likes to help singers and musicians by introducing them to managers, getting them chances to entertain in places where the pay is good. He's helped painters to sell pictures, and he's even gotten stories published for some of the writers who couldn't get started by themselves. You know what the old lady thinks of that. Commercialism. She says he's no true friend, that he's just preying on talented young black folks. According to her, his interest is just a passing fancy."

The room was very dim. The dancing was the slow orgiastic kind one finds in the den-like places that stay open till morning. Music was provided by a piano and a drum. Leander drank. Presently the small room took on a rosy glow. The loose-jointed dancers, humped at the shoulders and melting into their partners, delighted him more and more with their antics. But he was not satisfied to watch.

"Come on, gal," he said. "Let's rassle."

The drummer's cymbals clashed. His stick went into the air, touched the ceiling. His grinning upturned face was a rigid Congo mask.

Lottie hummed the melody softly as she danced. It seemed to Leander like the purring of a warm cat on his chest. The shadows of the room fell about him like pendulums of jungle vines. Dry, imaginary leaves crackled under his feet. Was this, he wondered, the primitive heritage that the old lady, Mrs. Rainwater, was trying to have him recapture? Hardly, he told himself. Hardly.

Meanwhile the telephone rang frantically in the hallway of the house where Leander had his room. The old black landlady, getting out of bed in her flannel night gown and stocking cap, answered petulantly.

"No, ma'am. Leander Holley ain't in yet. No'm, he ain't."

And when the boy returned at seven o'clock in the morning, he found a note. Mrs. Rainwater, it seemed, had called him at ten o'clock the night before, shortly after he left for Harlem. Failing to find him home, she had called again at every hour till three. Finally, she had left a message. Would Leander please call her as soon as he returned?

Mrs. Rainwater's voice, as calm and charming as ever, seemed nevertheless strange to Leander this morning.

"To Harlem with Lottie?" she said.

"Yes," he told her lightly. "The jungle beast in me raised his head and roared."

But she was not amused.

"I'd like to talk with you today."

"I'll come in the afternoon," he said respectfully. "Yes, ma'am."

Leander slept a few hours, but he was far from rested when he went to Larchmont. His head felt large, and his eyes burned, and his voice was husky. In addition, he was excited and apprehensive. He knew Mrs. Rainwater was displeased with his little jaunt, and he was not sure that she did not have a scolding in store. And when the Filipino butler let him in, Leander knew at once that all was not well in the Rainwater home. The atmosphere was charged. The boy felt more alien than ever before in the elegant surroundings. He walked with fear and trembling on the glassy floors.

Mrs. Rainwater was waiting in the sun parlor. She was rigid, as coldly beautiful as an old silver image. No blood ran in her veins, no passions stirred. The two exchanged casual words. Then Leander put the match to the powder.

"Where is Lottie?" he asked.

"She's gone home." The old woman's toe twitched ever so little. "I'll have to explain. I have put confidence in you youngsters, Leander. I have rested large hopes in you, your artistic development. Naturally I shouldn't want to be betrayed."

"Betrayed?"

"That's it exactly. At least *you* haven't gone that far

yet. Lottie didn't tell me the truth about that frolic of yours last night. She said she wasn't with you. I've had to discipline her. She's probably on her way to Philadelphia by now. Relatives of some sort, I think."

Leander could not speak. For a moment he saw his little golden world withdrawing, vanishing like an early moon behind foothills. He felt sick at the thought of such a loss. He wanted to cry. But in a moment he had another thought. Was it really because of Lottie's falsehood that she had been fired? Might it not have been to teach *Leander* a lesson—to let him know that the rules under which he now served were severe?

Resentment rose in him. She wants to make a slave of me, he thought. She wants me to get permission when I leave home. She's like the rest, like any other old miser—she's not giving something for nothing. Only her manners are different. She is refined.

"She didn't mean any harm—"

"Don't tell me that, Leander."

"Honestly, I suggested—"

"You suggested it, surely. But Lottie knew better. I've talked so much with her. She knew my attitude toward that licentious night life. It will cloud your ideals, throw you into contact with destructive influences. You met Tisdale?"

"Yes."

"See? That's what I mean. If you had only told me of your plans—"

"I'm sorry," he said. "I didn't think. I'm really sorry." He said it with conviction.

"Hm. Well—"

Leander couldn't get the episode out of his mind. If he had only told *her*—so that was it? He was to consult her, to get her approval when he wanted to leave his room. More and more resentment filled his mind. The loss of the tiny golden world became less and less a thing of dread. God, she regards me as a slave, he kept telling himself. I must have sold myself. For three days he did not touch a piano, did not sing a note. For the first time in a year he failed to go for his singing lesson at the appointed time.

"The devil with it," he said, and instead he spent the day walking in the country.

In the mail he found a note from Philadelphia, along with Mrs. Rainwater's letter. Lottie would be glad to have him come down—they might have another whirl together—but, of course, he knew the dangers. She was herself an object lesson to him. A single misstep might mean his losing the kingdom. Generous people like Mrs. Rainwater were not found every day. But if he did want to take a chance, she had something that might interest him. A well-established Negro quartet in that city had just lost its first tenor. The group was preparing for promising engagements in vaudeville (thanks to Tisdale, who was helping them) when a misfortune robbed them of one singer. Tisdale had recommended Leander to the manager.

Curiously, Mrs. Rainwater's letter dealt with the same subject, but in a different vein.

"Mr. Tisdale is seeking your address," it said. "He wants to tempt you into a vulgar quartet venture of some sort. Have nothing whatever to do with it."

The old woman knew everything, Leander thought. It

was almost mystic the way she got reports. He sat down and worked out a clever plot. He wrote Mrs. Rainwater a note in which he promised to have nothing to do with the quartet or with anything in which Mr. Tisdale was even remotely connected. He used all his most trusted blandishments to soothe the woman's feelings. Then in a postscript he remarked that he was running down to Philadelphia—simply for a change of air, a jaunt. He'd be back in two or three days. He *knew,* he said, she would approve, so he was not waiting for an answer.

In Philadelphia he purchased a lovely old bottle and sent it to her. He also wrote a letter each day while there; but when he returned he found no mail in his room, and consternation took him. He had offended the kind old woman, he thought. She was not angry or she would have written a sharp letter. She was just hurt, wounded. Leander's heart melted, and he hastened over to Larchmont with contrition on his lips, with words of apology ready.

Mrs. Rainwater had all his little absurd presents tied in a strong paper bundle that suggested an impending journey to the rubbish heap if he failed to call. She was standing when he entered the sun parlor.

"I didn't think you'd hope to fool me," she said.

"I—"

"It was positively brazen. That syrupy letter. The effrontery of it. Running down there, letting Tisdale and Lottie string you along—and to think that you would attempt to throw dust in my eyes. Traitors—"

"You can do what you please about it," Leander said pettishly. "You don't have to go on helping—"

"Do as I please!" And then, to his utter dismay, Mrs.

Rainwater stomped her small frail foot. "How can I recall those vocal lessons? How can I keep others from taking the credit for the talents I have sponsored. What can I do about that overcoat you're wearing?"

Leander's face burned. His hands became moist.

"I didn't ask for anything," he protested.

"You didn't directly—no, but you betrayed me into believing you had a soul."

He went out. On the quiet streets of the exclusive neighborhood he felt frightened. He had a strange presentiment that presently small, hostile children would come from behind those fine houses and pelt him with stones. He hurried.

At a corner drug store he entered a telephone booth and called Philadelphia. To Lottie he said, "Tell them that the quartet proposition will be O.K. I'll be down tomorrow."

HEATHEN AT HOME

One must remember that God's work is not the same as man's. Doing the work of God, for example, one has to be content with much smaller wages. Not that God pays more niggardly for his service, but in view of large compensations in the hereafter, meager salaries in the present are at least understandable. And, assured that he will withhold nothing, this is plainly the more profitable labor; yet the choosing of it wins the name of sacrifice.

It was as clear as two-times-two to Miss Abigale Conroy; she had made her choice deliberately and no doubt wisely. A large woman with hair more gray than black and a face that beamed with stalwart benignity, she looked back on twenty brave years in the vineyard and set her teeth for twenty more. Brave years! Yes, brave indeed they seemed to Miss Conroy, picking at her fingernails with the ivory letter knife and listening to the rattle of crisp red leaves at her window; and in recalling them she imagined that an almost imperceptible mist clouded the lenses of her horn-rimmed spectacles. Certainly she had no regrets and, as she often said, if she were starting her career again, she would select the same line of missionary endeavor.

Of course there were those who did not regard the work at Mount Lebanon as a missionary enterprise, but Miss Conroy had no patience with that view. She denounced it to her teachers in their little weekly faculty meetings; she gave it a powerful thrust once a year at the commencement exercises, and in her numerous lectures at clubs and churches she made her view eloquently convincing. The natives of Africa, she would explain, are no more superstitious, no more illiterate, no more benighted than are the poor blacks of Alabama. For this reason she had given up the hope of a professorship in a college in the Southwest. It is true that her position at Mount Lebanon had from the first offered an increased wage; but it closed a certain door of hope that led, Miss Conroy now felt, to fabulous earthly rewards. In other words she had made a personal sacrifice of the greatest sort to the cause of Negro education—all that she might have been had she continued as an instructor at the State Teachers' College she had given up. Her life, like a patriarchal lamb, was on the altar.

It was also true, though she minimized it now, at a distance of twenty years, that Miss Conroy could not have continued in her former teaching position anyway. An unsavory love affair, an absurd marriage, and a prompt separation had left her so humiliated that she had felt, at the time, on the brink of disgrace. This had been the prelude to a period of deep religious feeling, and Miss

Conroy had seized the call to Alabama as a direct answer to prayer. And in her new field, with the past forgotten, her courage had stood erect; she praised God for rescuing her by the skin of her teeth, loved the wretched black youngsters at her feet, and worked untiringly to build up the Mount Lebanon school.

Again she was not disappointed. Every stick Miss Conroy touched blossomed. Every stone she turned with her foot burst into singing. Around the little shack where she had conducted her first classes, there now stood a circle of handsome brick buildings. Where she and two assistants had once done all the teaching, there was now a staff of twenty men and women.

Miss Conroy did not attempt to suppress her pride; personal assurance, amounting almost to an attitude of ownership where Mount Lebanon was concerned, rose in her. This school was the work of her own hands. The buildings were all as she had dreamed them. The teachers, thanks to the depression and the consequent cheapness of academic degrees, were nearly all M.A.'s and Ph.D.'s. A few of the younger instructors were inclined to be godless, of course, but that was the influence of the times. She managed to keep them straight. And at the next meeting of the college board of trustees—mercy, she could hardly realize that the yearly meeting was only a week off!—she intended to recommend practically the entire staff for reappointment. Another brave year. Another year of victory in the midst of financial distress. Mount Lebanon would continue to catch a lot of students who were forced out of Fisk, Talladega, Wilberforce, and other more expensive schools. The trustees, sleepy and forgetful, would have their usual bouquets for the lady who stood at its head.

Life at Mount Lebanon had reached the point of tranquility for Miss Conroy. Her cozy and charming cottage was a symbol as well as an ornament on the campus. Indeed, until the present summer, there had been only one fly in Miss Conroy's ointment, only one strain on her contentment, her pride. *Now* there were two. But the first of these was old Homer Conroy.

In the year that business failed, Miss Conroy's brother Halleck wrote her from New York that he had gone to the wall. His little doll factory had collapsed like a matchbox in the general debacle. His son, Hal Jr., just finishing college in Texas, had no prospect of employment. As a result the ruined man was calling upon her—not to help him, of course, but to assume a certain family obligation that he had been quite willing to carry without aid as long as he had an income. Now life was all upset. Their uncle, Homer Conroy, was a very old man. He required constant care and attention. Could Abigale not send for him, since she had still a secure position, and keep him till the depression should lift?

Yes, Miss Conroy responded. Of course she would take Uncle Homer. She could not be sure how well the old man would enjoy life at Mount Lebanon, but that was not involved now. This was not a matter of choice. If her brother could no longer keep their frail uncle, the duty became hers. Miss Conroy was still on *her* feet. She went to the telephone, got Western Union, had a ticket wired, and calmly returned to the notes she was making for a chapel talk the next day.

But three days later, when the little gray man arrived, Miss Conroy was speechless. It was not that she couldn't believe her eyes—the person was real, cruelly real—but time and the years had played a horrid joke on poor old Uncle Homer. He stood at her door in a frayed overcoat fastened at the throat with a safety pin. In his left arm he clasped two immense loaves of bread from which the paper had been partly torn. He seemed unwashed.

"Uncle Homer!" she exclaimed.

"Lord, Abigale," he said. "I didn't know how you were fixed for things to eat, so I brought this bread along. Your brother never fed me enough. I would have died of starvation if I'd stayed there much longer. You're a long jaunt from the railroad, here." Again and again his little thin voice cracked like a china cup, it broke and shattered the words.

"Why, Uncle Homer, why didn't you phone?"

"I'm an independent man, and I can still walk if I have to," he told her. Then his thought flickered. "There are little better'n three hundred steps from the big road up here to your door. And Lord, look at all the trees. I wonder how many there are?"

"Don't count them now," she said.

A shower of bread crumbs fell on Miss Conroy's parlor rug. Suddenly she buried her face in her hands and began crying. One of the loaves slipped from the old man's arm, and tumbled under the grand piano. He did not notice the bread but seemed astonished and a bit impatient at the sight of her tears.

"Well, you're a right heap of a baby yet, I see. Seems

like they don't care much *who* they take for schoolteachers nowadays."

"Sit down, Uncle Homer. You need a rest." She recovered her strength. "I'm just a principal," she smiled. "They aren't so particular about them."

A tiny one-room cottage near the garage was renovated for the old man; and Nimrod, the black student who served Miss Conroy as yard boy, became his guardian. When the carpenters and painters finished their work, the place was neatly furnished and a discarded piano was secured for Uncle Homer's amusement. Miss Conroy came down to the flower bed where Nimrod was scratching the ground with a small fork.

"We'll probably have to get somebody else for this, Nimrod," she said. "I want you to give all your time to Uncle Homer. He'll need someone with him constantly. I've arranged to have a cot brought into the room so you can sleep right there."

The boy stood up, stretching the kink out of his back.

"Yes'm," he said. He wore overalls and the crown of a straw hat from which the brim had been torn.

"His mind is almost gone, Nimrod. He's no more than a baby, but he'll do what you tell him."

"H'm."

She continued down to the road and drove away in a roadster that stood by the gate. Nimrod shook the dirt from the roots of some Johnson grass he had pulled and gathered the sprigs into a box. The sky was splashed with gold beyond the pine trees.

That same evening the black boy lay on his new cot lamenting the job that had fallen to him. When he thought the old man was well asleep, he got up quickly and put out the light. It was the third time he had done it, but again the old man leaped from his bed and pulled it back on. Nimrod could not imagine why the man insisted on keeping a light, for he slept with his head under the cover; and Nimrod knew that Miss Conroy would have something to say if the night watchman reported a light in the cottage after ten o'clock. He turned on his cot in discomfort. Later he found a thread and tied it to the tiny brass chain in the electric fixture. Still Uncle Homer kept jumping up when Nimrod snapped the light, and continued to pull it on again. But there was a difference now. The old fellow gradually became frightened. He hadn't yet seen the thread.

"I wonder what makes that light keep going off," he said.

Nimrod chuckled to his pillow, but the next evening he had a harder problem.

Homer Conroy was not anxious to take a bath, had flatly refused in fact till Miss Conroy put down her foot and said, "Yes, Uncle Homer. You must let Nimrod bathe you. It is very necessary."

"Well," he said. "Maybe you're right, but I won't be bullied into it. I won't be bullied."

And Nimrod, leading the old man quietly to the tub, thought the difficulty was over. He washed Uncle Homer as best he could, then reached for the towels.

"You can step on the mat here," he said.

"Aw, let me stay in a little longer, Nimrod."

The old man was delighted by the warm water, the large tub. He splashed like a child, poured water on his head and let it run down his face. Nimrod waited with the towels in his hand and began to feel uneasy.

"You been in that warm water near 'bout half a hour," he said. "It ain't good to stay too long."

"Nonsense, Nimrod. It's only been a few minutes. Besides, it's the only pleasure that I get. Sit down awhile and rest yourself. I'm all right."

"H'm."

Nimrod racked his brain. A little later he fished the wash rag and the bar of soap from the water. In doing this he took pains to slip the stopper from the tub. Presently the old man noticed that something was happening.

"Why the water is just a-going, Nimrod."

"You musta kicked the stopper out."

"The stopper? Oh, where is it?"

He began searching the water with his fingers. By the time he found it, the water was gone.

"You'd better let me dry you, Mr. Conroy. You'll catch cold," Nimrod said.

The old man stepped out sadly.

"It's all the pleasure I get," he murmured.

"It ain't good to stay too long, though."

The next morning Uncle Homer walked into the students' chapel exercises with his hat on, and the young folks giggled so persistently that Miss Conroy had to step down from the platform and remove it for him. In the afternoon he wandered across the hill to the school farm where a group of boys were hitching mules to plows. His round, baby-blue eyes swept the landscape.

"All this land belongs to my niece Abigale," he said suddenly. He saw the black boys roll their eyes and smile, but he continued, "You don't seem to understand. This place belongs to Abigale. These are Abigale's mules, and all of you are Abigale's niggers."

Several of the boys winced. Nimrod came up the path, took the old man by the arm and led him away.

That evening, when he had tucked Uncle Homer in bed, Nimrod walked around the campus to the boys' dormitory. The lights were out, and the students should have been in bed. About a dozen of them had disregarded the rule, however; they had gathered in a room at the end of the hall on the top floor. They wore pajamas; and their eyes, in all parts of the dark room, were round with excitement. Nimrod flopped on the bed beside two or three others. The boys were talking slightly above whispers. Nimrod knew all their voices.

"You heard him, didn't ya, Baron?"

"Sure. I don't believe it just popped outta his head, neither."

"You daggone right it didn't. He picked that up round home."

"Now you're talking, Splink." This was a third voice. "He 'bout heard Abigale calling us niggers, talking 'bout *her* this and *her* that—like if she owned the place. She ain't foolin' me."

Behind closed doors the students sometimes disrespectfully referred to Miss Conroy by her first name.

"Tell 'em 'bout it, Andy," Nimrod said. "She's been scairt he'd spill the beans ever since he hit the place—makes me keep him cooped up like a baby."

"He ain't as crazy as he makes out," Baron said.

"The old lady's been around here too long," Splink suggested. "She thinks she owns this place sho nuff. She thinks this is her plantation. You notice how she dismisses you from class whenever they need some work done on the farm? I see through it. I can see through some of them chapel talks of hers too: that line 'bout how good it is for a fellow to be here even if he have to work near all his way and can't take but one study a year. That's just what she wants. She ain't bothered 'bout y-all learning nothing; she just wants to make good niggers outa you."

"She's done a lot for the school," Nimrod compromised. "She's built it up a lot."

"She ain't done nothing for me," Baron said. "She ain't done nothing but touched a lot of rich white folks for money. Took us all over the country singing and raising collections."

"And another thing," Splink said, "did you ever hear 'bout anybody keeping count of that money? I traveled with the quartet two years, and I ain't never heard tell of no kind of honest-to-goodness report. I seen many a person slip her a twenty or a hundred or more and she just stuffed it in her pocketbook. When we got back, she'd say, 'Well, the quartet raised such an' such a 'mount.' There never was no real 'count kept."

That was a stunning intimation. Nimrod gasped to think that anyone could entertain such a thought about Miss Conroy. Yet, he reasoned, it was not impossible, and if she was indifferent to their learning, if she called them niggers behind their backs, if she had come to feel she owned the school, anything was possible. Still Nimrod did not believe she was deliberately dishonest. If she kept poor accounts, it was hardly for personal gain. He suspected now that she held scorn and contempt for her black students, but he was not certain whether this was her fault or theirs. The way they groveled at her feet, bowing and scraping to please her whims, must have been disgusting.

"She ain't been here twenty years for nothing," Andy said. "You heard her talk about how many other jobs she turned down, didn't you? Well now, hating us the way she does, there must be some other reason why she's so glad to stay. And I can see now what it is."

"I don't reckon it's the money so much; she gets enough to live on," Nimrod mused. "Yet and still, she do get a heap of service. She gets more service than some millionaires. Then she travels all over the country—she loves that. She gets to meet high-toned people that she couldn't hardly wash dishes for if she wasn't s'posed to be some kinda know-all on black folks. I *know* she loves that."

Nimrod saw from the dormitory window that Uncle Homer had the light on again in the cottage, so he left the group promptly. On his cot a few moments later he tossed in an agony of confused thoughts, warring sentiments. He felt personally devoted to Miss Conroy; she had picked him up on the streets of Birmingham and revived his interest in life, given him a new vision. Now the devil was telling him that it was not a genuine interest in his welfare that had rescued him, that the lady really hated him. Well, at least it was something to think about. He would have to keep his eyes open.

In less than a week he discovered the conclusive evidence in Miss Conroy's wastebasket. Nimrod had not sought unduly for it. The word simply rose from the page, assailed his eyes of its own will. It was there as plain as day, in her own handwriting on a discarded letter she had begun to her brother. "Of course, you will understand my humiliation," it read, "with two hundred giggling darkeys pointing their black fingers at me while Uncle Homer cavorts about the place. It is simply impossible for him to stay longer, Halleck."

Nimrod folded the paper without emotion and deposited it in his pocket. So that was it. She was telling her brother to relieve her of Uncle Homer and the other part just slipped out. Giggling darkeys. Pointing their black fingers. It was too clear. She hated them. She hated them more than she could even express to her brother.

Miss Conroy raised the blinds of her living room to the morning sun. The autumn trees were lovely on the campus. The boys were marching around the circle to the dining hall. They smiled but their faces were not hopeful. They were a well-disciplined lot, respectful, orderly, humble. The way they observed the rule about not crossing the campus lawn was typical of their behavior, typical of their respect for Miss Conroy and for her authority. It did her good to see them march half around the circle when they could have saved nearly a city block by cutting directly across. Now and again perhaps some reckless youngster, late for his meal, would dart under the trees if he thought no one was looking. But that was rare, and a few words from Miss Conroy would cure the offender for life. Thus more was preserved than simply the grass on the campus. For the first time in several weeks the principal of the Mount Lebanon school wore a genuine smile.

The gladness on Miss Conroy's face, however, was compounded of more elements than those visible from her window. Into it went something that had nothing to do with the beauty of the campus or the discipline of her students. Uncle Homer was on a fast train that by this time should be puffing into Washington and by afternoon would reach New York. The poor, dear man, so wasted and helpless, so naive and childish. He excited love as well as pity, but he could never remain at Mount Lebanon. The situation was peculiar here. He caused her great embarrassment during his brief stay. If allowed to remain he might in time wreck the work of her twenty years. Fortunately Halleck had understood her explanation. He had consented to take the old man back. Yet, Miss Conroy remembered soberly, the terms of the agreement were not easy. She had promised to find a job for Hal Jr. at Mount Lebanon. It would be annoying to explain such a move to the board of control. Hiring additional teachers at a time like the present might look a bit odd in view of shrunken budgets; and when the new teacher happened to be your own nephew, it became doubly strange. Miss Conroy's smile vanished. A second fly marred the ointment.

The new situation did not call for worry, however. Miss Conroy's relations with the Board had always been delightful. The sober men and women who came to the annual meeting had gainsayed her nothing in twenty years. Even when she had asked to have one of their number removed because his support seemed lukewarm, they had bowed gravely and crushed the offending gnat. In the present situation, Miss Conroy was embarrassed to imagine what some members might *think*. What they would say and do she could foretell. So there was no deep cause for worry.

Frances was frying eggs in the kitchen. A moment later the glossy brown girl came to the door and told Miss Conroy that breakfast was ready.

"Yes, yes. Dear me, I haven't time to be mooning here at the window."

Before she had finished eating, the girl returned.

"Nimrod's at the do'," she said. "He want to know can he speak to you a minute."

"Yes, of course. Tell him to come in."

The boy was dressed for school. He held in his hand a comical little cap he wore on the campus.

"I was gonna tell you," he said, "the boys is kinda upset."

"Yes? It doesn't seem to affect their appetites. I saw them going to breakfast a few moments ago."

Nimrod smiled, bowed his head sheepishly.

"I reckon not," he said. "Yet and still there's a heap o' funny talk."

"Funny talk?"

"Yes'm."

"Talk about what?"

"The boys ain't satisfied with the new p'fessor."

Miss Conroy snapped aggressively, her face taking a deep red.

"The *boys* not satisfied! Are the boys running the school?"

"Oh, no ma'm. I didn't go to say it like that. They ain't trying to run things, and they ain't trying to show you how. I just thought I'd tell you what I heard 'em say."

She waited a moment. Then she spoke in another key.

"What is it they're saying about Hal?"

"Yesterday," Nimrod began, "some of the boys was working in the new building. Mr. Conroy came through. They wa'n't working fast enough to suit him, so he told them he was gonna put a end to some of the damn loafing—and off he starts toward yo' office, like as if he's fixing to report it to you. The boys say he's the first teacher ever to talk to them like that, and they thought that beingst he's yo' nephew—"

"Listen, Nimrod, do you expect me to believe Professor Conroy said that?"

He shrugged his shoulders.

"I don't know, ma'am."

Again she boiled.

"Well, frankly, Nimrod, I think it's a lie."

The boy trembled as he backed away. From the door he saw Miss Conroy sitting very rigid in her chair, an empty coffee cup held absentmindedly in one hand. She was not usually caustic with students. Her left toe tapped the floor rapidly. Nimrod was sorry he had tried to tell her what the boys were saying. She was about to have a fit just over that little. And he had only begun to tell her what was really in their minds. Lordy! What if he had told her all, *everything?* She would find out though, and she'd find out soon. And how she would explode! Whowee!

Nimrod gathered up the books he had left on the back steps and hurried to class.

At her front window again, Miss Conroy looked across the campus with troubled eycs. The Board members were already arriving. Two of the guest rooms had been occupied the past night. The other members could be expected within a few hours. Miss Conroy looked at her watch. She was ready for breakfast a few minutes earlier than usual. She hated to admit to herself that she felt a trifle uneasy at the prospect of a Board meeting, that she had a presentiment of some slight embarrassment at the session. Yet, it was true.

Poor Hal. Her thought turned to the young manual training teacher, her nephew. How atrocious of the boys to invent such a report about him. Why even a student would be dismissed for using *damn's* on the Mount Lebanon grounds. It was unthinkable. The place was consecrated, a Christian school. Hal could not have forgotten that. He had probably reproved an indolent youngster a bit harshly. Nothing more. Surely Hal was not idiot enough to make such a break before she could even get his appointment approved. The boys' thoughts were running to nonsense. She would have to change their daily program, have the rising bell rung a half hour earlier.

Frances was at the door.

"Miss Conroy—"

At the same instant Miss Conroy saw something on the campus that paralyzed her muscles. She stood like a pillar of salt at the drawn curtain. Frances was saying something, but Miss Conroy did not hear another word. Her face turned to a hideous mask. She gasped. The fingernails bit into the flesh of her palms.

"Miss Conroy—" Frances repeated.

The boys were crossing the campus, hurrying directly across, *walking on the lawn*. They were walking abreast instead of in file as usual, and there was something military and menacing about the way they slipped under the trees. Not one or two boys—all of them were brazenly tramping across the grass. Was it an affront to school regulations?—to Miss Conroy? What on earth did they mean? Didn't they know there were members of the school board already in the guest rooms?—that some of these were probably looking at this demonstration? It occurred to Miss Conroy that the boys were not going to the dining hall. Dear God, what did this mean? She ran to another window and saw them gathering under a large oak in front of the auditorium. The girls were coming now. The group began singing *Stay in the Field till the War is Ended.* What kind of rally would they choose to hold at the breakfast hour? Miss Conroy began to feel giddy. She snatched her hat and rushed down the path and up the road.

She reached the scene in time to hear a student orator say: "We'll have perfect order throughout the strike." A strike! How dreadful! Yet, curiously, Miss Conroy's poise began to return. She listened with a calmness that amazed the young Negroes while the plan was outlined. "We'll place student monitors at the doors of each building. No one will do any work or attend any classes till we get a hearing from the Board. We intend to present our cause direct. In the meantime we can pack our trunks and get ready to go back home if that's necessary."

"How 'bout them what ain't got no home to go to back?" someone cried.

"Pack your trunk just the same," the speaker said. "The committee will work out the details and let you know the next move."

There followed a number of pep speeches in which

many students asserted that they would hang together till hell froze, or nearly that long. In the midst of these they paused to sing another spiritual.

Miss Conroy listened a good while, then walked away leisurely and with calm dignity.

"Today he had a pistol in his pocket," Nimrod murmured in a drowsy voice. His gaze was on the carpeted floor, and his large hands bulged his coat pockets. He was so shy in the presence of the gray-bearded board members that he could scarcely be heard. Yet his words fell like drops of melted lead on the prim old men, the devout women. Instantly they straightened in their chairs, their eyes blinked, and a gasp of astonishment passed around the sedate circle like an electrical current transmitted at the elbows.

A pistol! A weapon of death in the sacred precincts. Had they lived to see the desecration of Mount Lebanon, these veterans of service? Was it literally true that this temple of love, built in tears by bruised hands, had commenced to crumble? Or was this, as seemed more likely, the hysterical mouthing of a black boy who wasn't very bright?

Nimrod took his seat in the corner with the six other members of the student committee. There was an intense silence. All the other things that the students had said in thc two-hour session were forgotten, all their petty complaints about the food, the campus regulations, about little racial degradations practiced by some members of the white faculty—suddenly they all seemed unimportant, and for the first time the board members took the situation seriously.

"It's fantastic," Miss Conroy said. She rose from her chair, took a few padded steps on the rich carpet, and raised both hands like claws above her shoulders. "Fantastic," she repeated, and the sounds hissed through her clenched teeth.

The chairman, a philanthropic banker from the Midwest, cleared his throat.

"I dare say it is," he said. "Yet we really should clear this point. No doubt these students are sincere. They probably *imagine* that Mr. Conroy had a . . . a . . . pistol. And this would be a horrible rumor to sow. It would reflect on the principal of the school as well as on the teacher. I think that all these young people need is the assurance that their suspicions are unfounded, and they will instantly fall into line and co-operate to the fullest." He beamed on the students with an awkward smile, but they did not raise their eyes. "Let's call in Mr. Conroy."

"That's not really necessary," Miss Conroy said. "It is not necessary to take the position that teachers are responsible to the students. And this thing is too absurd to warrant serious attention. We need to discipline some of the students who are leading out in the movement. There's been nothing like it, nothing so insolent, in the twenty years—"

"Yes, that's probably true," the chairman said. "But if we go more than half way and call in Mr. Conroy, I think that will serve to pour oil on the troubled waters. It will hush the ugly rumors—and really I'd hate to have them reach the people whose money we rely on for support."

One of the ladies on the board, a former missionary who wore a long white linen dress and a high black hat, supported Miss Conroy. But a large man with yellow hair turned the tide. He was president of a Southern white college, and he favored calling the young man in. This would even be the best course for Miss Conroy. Otherwise the students would conclude that she condoned the act.

Halleck Conroy was a powerful fellow with short black hair parted on the side. His nose had been broken in a football game, and he seemed a bit more rugged than the other persons in the room. Yet he was gentle when he answered the chairman's question.

"Yes," he said slowly. "I had a pistol today."

There was a black silence. Then a long pause. The chairman was first to recover.

"But surely you were not carrying it with intent to injure?"

"I don't know," the young man said honestly. "It was like a mutiny here. The students took control of the kitchen, put guards at the buildings, and refused to recognize the authority of the teachers. I didn't know what might happen; I'm new here. Aunt Abigale told me it was all on account of me; so I thought I'd better be careful. I've been carrying this all day."

He held the pistol in his palm.

"That wasn't necessary, Conroy," the chairman said. "Leave that here."

The pistol lay on the desk when the young teacher left. Miss Conroy buried her face, crying heavily. The lady missionary consoled her and put an arm around her shoulder.

"What was it the students were asking for?" a very old man asked.

The secretary consulted her notes.

"They want a new principal; they want the teacher replaced who was removed when Mr. Conroy was hired; they want several campus rules rescinded, and they want better food."

Again there was a pause, an emptiness.

"Well," the chairman finally said. "I think we can assure these young people that we have their interests at heart, that we will do the very best thing for them. And if they will take up their work as usual tomorrow, they may be confident that the board will at least study their needs at the proper time. Nothing can be done in a hurry, of course."

The seven students filed out. They were smiling, but their faces were not hopeful.

Miss Conroy was still crying in the missionary's arms.

THE DEVIL IS A CONJURER

❦

The dogs gathered around the trunk of a solitary oak on a clearing and set up a monstrous chorus. The tired, breathless Negroes came lumbering down the hillside like steers. Beaver was near the front, his hand perspiring from the grip he had taken on his stick. There was a moment of pause in the midst of the din. The boy noticed that the men, King and Sam, were looking into the tree, rapt. When Beaver looked up, he understood. He saw something that gave him a jolt. There was a dark, shadowy creature almost as large as a yearling heifer. But it was no yearling; it was a tree-climbing animal and it was hanging out near the end of a strong bough.

There was no time to talk. The dogs were howling furiously. Beaver knew his job and he took his place below the tree and waited for Sam and King to boost him up to the first limb. They gave what help they could, and in another moment the wiry boy was high in the boughs, clinging firmly and lashing out with his stick at the thing on the end of the branch. The creature—Beaver never got a clear view of it—was remarkably stubborn, but after a time, with the boy's stick thrashing through the leaves, the thing backed away, edged away blindly on its limb, lost its grip, and dropped to the ground.

In the same second all the dogs pounced. Then, for some amazing reason, they all became silent. They sniffed at the spot where the creature had landed and began running around in circles. Sure as judgment day, the "coon" was gone—disappeared—vanished. The dogs kept sniveling around the tree and looking more and more shamefaced.

The clearing and the slope were as distinct in the moonlight as they could have been by day, but that ghostly varmint had vanished like smoke. The dogs failed to set a tooth in him. Beaver slipped down the tree stem and followed the dumbfounded crowd home. There wasn't much to talk about as they walked. It was a time to get a quilt and cover one's head.

Well, suh, Beaver meditated while walking, you can say what you is pleased to say, sweet peoples, you can do what you is bound to do, but big boy Beaver ain't with you no mo'. I ain't skeered of a living thing what's really something, but I doesn't aim to mess round wid a devilish something what ain't nothing. I likes to hear a hound dog yawl, and I likes to shake a coon out a tall tree, do he climb one. That's all well and good. Mighty fine, I *thank* you. Yet and still—

The little crowd came over a knoll to a line of cabins nesting under tulip trees. Without the exchange of words, understanding had passed between them. It was a time to get indoors, shove something heavy in front of the door, wrap one's head in a quilt. Beaver knew as well as the others. He found his own door, closed it behind him, braced it securely.

It wasn't only that the dogs had treed a phantom which disappeared when they pounced upon it. That was enough, Lord knows, but queer things had been happening for weeks on the Greenbrier Plantation. At first, sheep and hogs had vanished without explanation. Later there was the incident of Mr. Bob Leslie's German police dog. This fine animal, capable of whipping a pack of common hound dogs, had been slain mysteriously, his head and shoulders left under a tree on the knoll, his body gone.

The Greenbrier Negroes could stand only so much mystery. And Beaver, who was still a boy, knew when his cup was full. When morning came, he stretched his legs on the hard ground under the bed, tightened the quilt over his head, but made no move to come out.

He was alone in the cabin. Granny, his only guardian, had spent the night across the branch, as she often did, helping to birth a baby on the Beasley place. Beaver said his prayers over and over again, but it didn't help his courage.

Somewhat later there was the clatter of a horse's hooves outside and a gruff voice shouting.

"What in the name of God's come over you all—gone crazy?"

Beaver uncovered his head, crept to the door, opened it a crack.

"Nah, suh, Mistah Cap'n Bob. Us ain't gone crazy—leastwise, not plum."

The white man stiffened on his saddle. The red in his

cheeks brightened. He spat, not minding where, and fixed his teeth as if to bite. Beaver had reason to quake, but his experiences of the past night had left him numb.

"It's near about noon, black boy."

"Yes, suh, it is for a fact."

"The mules ain't had a bite to eat."

"Nah, suh."

"I don't see no ball and chain tied to your feet, and I know you ain't paralyzed."

"I been studying about that old something or ruther what kilt yo' fine police dog, Mistah Bob. Now that were mo'n a caution how that police dog of yo's got kilt."

"Listen. I'll give you ten minutes to be in the field, Beaver. You and all the rest."

"You better see King and Sam and 'em, Mistah Cap'n Bob. I don't think us'll be there in no ten minutes, though. No ten hour neither."

A few minutes later, however, most of the Negroes were standing in a huddle in front of the cabin row. They formed a compact circle around Bob Leslie and his tall horse, and the overseer soon heard a stirring account of the phantom of the past night. He heard the excited Negroes link it with the killing of his dog, the loss of his sheep and hogs.

Leslie knew as well as they that there was a monstrous thing abroad. If there had been any doubt in his mind about the sheep and hogs he had lost, the manner in which his police dog had been killed put the thing beyond speculation. But he couldn't admit that the whole situation was reason for a general holiday. For once, however, the black folks would not be driven. Neither would they respond to soft words.

"They's heap mo' to it what you don't know, suh," King ventured.

They gave it to Cap'n Bob, bit by bit. Someone had seen a vague, misty thing leaping tall fences, running like the light, crossing fields, slipping through hedges and clumps, seen it clearly just after daybreak on a recent morning. Another had been surprised by a creature which he described as a pale, spotted kangaroo. It had just cleaned out his chicken roost and was bounding like the very ghost of peril toward the dark wooded hills.

"Nah, suh, I don't reckon us'll be going to the fields right soon," Sam told the overseer.

Bob Leslie rode away without answering, but he had his own thoughts.

By afternoon he had alarmed the countryside for miles around. Whether a bear, a panther, a lion, or a spotted kangaroo, he could not say, but certainly there was a varmint abroad that threatened the peace of a quiet farming community in northern Alabama. The black folks refused to take the lead in a systematic search, but perhaps if a posse of white men, men possessing arms, could be organized, the others would follow. That is how Leslie figured it out in his own mind; that is how he told it to his neighbors, and he was not wrong.

When evening came Beaver joined the men who had gathered with King and Sam in the wagon shed. They trimmed a lantern wick and King raised his leg and struck a match on the seat of his pants. Carrying the little flame between them, the two older fellows led the way up to the line of cabins. Beaver walked behind, his heart pumping.

"Come on out Jimboy. You Primus! Zeke—come on, y'-all."

They gathered quickly. In the big road the group was met by Leslie and the company of white neighbors he had assembled. A dozen large police dogs stood at their heels. Guns were passed out. There were not enough to go around. Beaver managed to get his hands on the last, an antique affair, uncommonly heavy.

"There ain't but one place to look for the varmint—whats'n'ever it is," Leslie said. "He's bound to be back in them woods if he's anywheres hereabouts."

"H'm," King murmured, his great nostrils dilating.

"You done said it all, Mistah Cap'n Bob," Beaver piped. "He is duty bound to be in them woods somewheres—do you ask me."

"Hush, Beaver. And quit that trembling, too. Now let's spread out some. We got enough here to have three groups. Long's we stay in hollering distance to the next one we're all right."

"H'm. Mmmm!" The murmur passed around the circle.

Leslie made the separation. In his own crowd he took King and Sam and Beaver. One group took the road that circled the hill to the right. The second went left, proposing to cut back across a hay field. Beaver saw that his crowd had already started through the old peach orchard and that Leslie was keeping the dogs together.

They went along quietly for a space. The immense dogs ran ahead, barking very little, a trifle uncertain, but ready for anything.

"They doesn't run like coon dogs," Beaver observed.

"No, they *ain't* coon dogs," Sam answered.

"How you say that varmint looked, Beaver?"

"I tell you, Mistah Bob, I didn't get a real good look whilst I was whupping him down from that tree. You see, I made so sure he was just a big old overgrown coon, I just didn't pay much 'tention. But Sam is the one what seen him in the light."

"You reckon what you seen was the same thing, Sam?"

"Musta been, Mistah Bob," Sam whispered. "The way how it was skimming over fences, near 'bout flying, make me think it couldn't a-been nothing else, suh. It wa'n't a natchal varmint, Mistah Bob."

Beaver began stuttering again. He was trembling again. "Th-th-th-th-th—"

"Mind out," King told him. "You'll bite off yo' tongue directly."

"Catch your breath a minute. Now, what are you trying to say?"

"About these guns. I been wondering 'bout these guns, Mistah Bob. Beingst that ain't no natchal varmint—beingst it's a hant-like—"

"Hush. It eats, don't it? It likes young sheep, don't it? It's bound to be one thing or the other. If it's a varmint, guns'll do the work. If it's a spirit—well, that's something else."

"What you make out of the way it disappeared and all, Mistah Bob?"

"You niggers is always visioning, Beaver. Just half of what you see is real."

They could hear the others now and again, their voices floating on the quiet night like the drone of insects. And sometimes, when these sounds came, Beaver felt a quick shiver that was not fear at all, a shiver that was more like coon-hunting excitement. But, Lordy, this was a fearful hunt! Beaver even felt sorry for the big powerful police dogs, venturing ahead, poking their noses into dark clumps, not knowing when they were likely to meet the thing they were all seeking.

After an hour of tramping the dogs became noisy and presently jumped an animal that circled a time or two in a clearing, selected a tree, and scampered up to the highest bough.

King narrowed his little shoe-button eyes.

"H'm," he said. "They's playing with something down yonder."

"Didn't run much, did it?" Leslie noticed.

Sam shook his head slowly.

"Something kinda tells me they's messing wid the *real* trouble, too. Them barks don't sound just right."

"Holler to the others," Leslie said. "Don't go too fast."

"Hee-oo!" Beaver called. "Hee-oo-oo!"

The three groups converged near the tree. By that time the dogs were almost mad, leaping into the air, running up the trunk, frothing bitterly.

No one spoke for a moment. It wasn't easy to make out the creature clearly. Half hidden by leaves, dim, dark, shadowy—it might have been anything. Would it vanish presently? How could it be so complacent? Could the thing actually be unafraid?

Leslie and his white neighbors put their heads together but said nothing. The Negroes began sighting down the barrels of their guns.

"Humph! It *do* look que'r enough," one of the white men thought. "By golly, I never heard tell of a varmint crossed with a hant, but yet and still, you can't always tell."

"Better feed him a few buckshots," Leslie suggested. "Come on, y'-all. Let's let him have it."

King got down on one knee, sighting carefully. Sam steadied his barrel against a sapling. Two of the white men took a few paces backwards. The dogs were in a hopeless confusion around the trunk of the tree. Beaver did not take his gun off his shoulder.

"Won't do no good, Mistah Bob," he said. "King and 'em can tell you the same thing, suh. I whupped that varmint out of a tree 'long here last night, but when he tetched the ground, that ended it. The hound dogs made a leap at him but they didn't bite a thing. That ain't a natchal varmint."

"Hush, Beaver. Let's see what y'-all can do now. There. . . ."

Six or eight guns squeezed off together.

Varmint or hant, pale creature or spotted—there was a momentary turmoil among the upper leaves of the tree. A bough was broken. It began to sag. Snatching, clawing, whining, the "thing" was losing its hold. Beaver stood with his mouth wide open and tried to endure the moment it takes for a shot creature to fall. The breath was completely out of the boy. Then, with a jolt, he realized that the varmint was actually tumbling . . . down . . . down.

"Oop-oop!" Beaver cried.

"He ain't dead," King said.

The creature struck the ground, and the dogs pounced. Then suddenly one dog was hurled back. They pounced again and the vicious creature struck a second police dog, killing it with a single lash. Was it a mortal varmint? Beaver began crying aloud. The men huddled together in little quaking groups. The dogs pounced again and the tide turned. The men ventured near, step by step.

"Well, dog my cats," King said.

When they pulled the dogs off, the creature was still breathing. It was a giant bobcat. Shot down by no less than six bullets, mortally wounded, it had yet managed to snuff the life out of two powerful police dogs before it died.

"There's your hant, Sam," Leslie said.

Sam stood shaking his head above the thing. He stood there a long time. Finally he said, "I ain't so sure this here's the thing what I seen, Mistah Bob."

Some of the men laughed together. Beaver stood apart, his face downcast.

"Listen, boy," Leslie said to him, "if you've got a good aim, you can always find out whether a varmint is crossed with a hant or not."

Beaver wasn't glad to hear it. He had momentarily a curious, foolish feeling. Perhaps there were no more hants around. Maybe the devil was no longer working his conjure. Surely it was sad to contemplate a wood like this, so fine and big, in which there were no more hants, no creatures immune to hurt and death.

Beaver smiled faintly.

"Ya-suh, Mistah Cap'n Bob," he said.

LET THE CHURCH ROLL ON

Four dusky elders, dark-clad but wearing milk-white girdles and turbans, marched up and down the aisles keeping step with the singing. The sermon had been long, fervent, and frequently unintelligible; but now, thanks the Lord, that part was over, and the footwashing ordinance could be celebrated presently.

The church seethed like an oven. Every bench was filled tight. Extra seats had been placed along the walls in the balcony and downstairs in the space near the rostrum. All available standing room was occupied. There were even faces on the outside, bobbing above the window sills. Every black man and his brother was at Mount Pleasant.

No, it wouldn't be long now. Some of the worshipers commenced changing their positions, vacating whole pews so that alternate benches could be turned around to face the ones just behind. The changes were made slowly, almost solemnly, yet there was much fanning during the interval, many trips to the open windows, and not a little expectorating.

Meanwhile, however, it wasn't right to let the spirit die. The elders marched steadily, droning as they went. A bevy of dark sisters, buxom, white-clad, and crisply starched, rose and joined the procession. They wore little white caps, and their broad posteriors bobbed piously as they walked; their feet ached and their bones creaked, but it wasn't right to let the spirit die. Soon their voices drowned out the voices of the elders whom they followed up the right aisle, across the back, down the left, across the front, and back up the right. The whole church took up the murmur and the room vibrated to the rafters. Now and again a strong throat hurled out a few distinct words.

I am climbing Jacob's ladder, ladder;
I am climbing . . .

The small beige pastor, lonesome and lost in an oversized Prince Albert, left the pulpit limp and exhausted. His wilted collar was no more than a rag around his neck. He was still mopping his face with a purple handkerchief; but his head was bowed now, as if he wept, and large fanlike hands kept opening and closing before his face. Clear black lines edged his darting fingernails. He was moving toward a rear door; in passing, however, he paused and whispered something into a pricked ear. It wasn't right to let the spirit die. Keep them chilluns warm, brother.

The prick-eared brother immediately smote his hands together like cymbals, opened his mouth, and gave the song a boom fit to break the windows.

Every round goes higher, higher;
Every round goes . . .

Dink Bowser, standing outside the door with his legs crossed, saw the distressed look on the preacher's face and leaned forward sympathetically. When he was within reaching distance, he put out his hand and caught the sleeve of the little man's exceptionally large swallowtail.

"Rev'm Lissus," he said. "That was powerful preaching you done, suh."

"Was I sure 'nough preaching, Brother Dink?"

"Preaching? Great God a-mussy, you was near about walking on air, Rev'm! But howcome you looks worried? Howcome you looks worried and whispers in old Moon Dawson's ear when you come past him just now?"

"I tell you, Dink, I'm going out here to rest myself in the woodshed whilst they's changing things up for the foot-washing, but I'm worried about them chilluns."

"Aw, don't study about them, Rev'm. Jesus Christ hisself couldn't do nothing with these here young-uns now-days. They's too full of devilment to get religion."

The little pale brown preacher wrinkled his brow, pondering. Before he answered, he went to the corner spiggot and took a drink. He wiped his mouth with the back of his hand.

"I'm *'bliged* to study about them, Brother Dink. They's been moaning all day, all this morning and all this afternoon, sitting there on the bench with they heads hanging down, and if they don't come through and get religion, folks'll blame me. They'll say I wa'n't preaching."

"Aw, no, Rev'm. Eve'body know about these devilish kids."

"Listen, Dink. You help keep them warm whilst things is getting changed round for the ordinances—will you?"

Dink was willing to do what he could but he was afraid

that wouldn't be much; and besides he wasn't too hopeful about these kids. Till now his interest in the church services, even in those so special as footwashing, had been decidedly objective. Dink was the caretaker of the building. And while he was also a member, it was his duty to sweep the aisles, pick up trash, and put things in order for the next meeting, and Dink was looking ahead. He knew from long experience just how much water got splashed during an ordinance like this one, and it was not easy for him to banish these thoughts and surrender himself to the spell. It would be somewhat like a bartender getting drunk on his job, or a cook stuffing himself with the food he's preparing for others. But now he had given Rev'm Lissus his word. He slipped through the crowd and wormed himself into a front seat between two deacons.

H'm, he reflected, craning his neck and taking in the whole room. Surely this was as big a crowd as Mount Pleasant had ever held. The alternate benches had all been turned and the worshipers were settling down in their new places. It had not taken long. They were only on the second song. The elders, followed by the whiteclad sisters, were just making their third round of the aisles. And those who had gone outside for a dip of snuff, a taste of whiskey, or a breath of fresh air were returning now. Two brothers stood in the back door with pans and towels; another followed with buckets of water.

The song droned on. When he listened attentively, Dink imagined he could hear throbs like pulse-beats. But that didn't matter. It proved one thing, however. There were some members with modern notions who thought the church needed a piano to give the singing "body." Dink had no patience with such Christians. Why, he'd just as soon hear somebody picking a guitar in church as playing a piano. He could still thank the Lord that Mount Pleasant hadn't yet been corrupted.

Suddenly the children flashed into his mind again. How about them, anyway? Did they show any signs of coming through? Or were they just naturally too devilish ever to get religion? He raised his eyes and looked across at the moaners' bench.

There were seven of them sitting there and only one, a boy as scrawny as a stringbean, could touch the floor with his feet. All held their chins in their hands and rolled their eyes at one another now and again. Two of the little girls were evidently twins; they wore identical bright red dresses. Their hair, short and obstinate, had been plaited from front to back in the old corn-roll fashion, the little ropes lying flat against the skull and seeming to run from the forehead to the nape of the neck. At the end of the bench a small boy had rested his elbow on the arm of the seat and had become almost too comfortable for his own good; his mouth had dropped open and his eyes were plainly heavy.

Dink looked at them one by one, wondering. What about these devilish kids? Wasn't Rev'm Lissus fretting himself too much on account of them? Would they ever get happy and come through? It was surely a hard job Rev'm had cut out for himself. Dink felt sorry for the little preacher in the oversized Prince Albert.

Of course, you never could tell about religion. Sometimes the spirit worked awful peculiar. Look a-there, old Mose Sanders spitting on the floor again—plague take him!

Yes, anything *could* happen when the spirit walked. No need speculating on that, sweet peoples. God's hand never was a bit short. Yet and still, them kids must of been a powerfully discouraging sight to a preacher. There, that little black brat had gone plum asleep. Look at him—near about sliding off the bench.

The pans were all placed and the water poured. There was one pan at each bench, sitting in the aisle at the left, and beside it a clean white towel. The elders sat down piously on the front seat and began removing their shoes.

Shall Jesus bear the cross alone
And all the world go free?

Rev'm Lissus returned from the woodshed. He took his place between the visiting preachers who sat with him in the pulpit. A fat lemon-colored man with carrot-colored hair stepped down to the rail and knelt to pray. The peals rose to the rafters, a soft sensuous thunder. Then lightning struck; someone screamed in the Amen corner.

"Glory!"

No, there's a cross for every one,
And there's a cross for me.

When the tide ebbed, the lemon-colored preacher cleared his throat and began.

"Ummm. Ummmmmmmm-a. Oh, Lord, Lord-Lord! Ummmm-a . . . We praise and bless thy name-a. . . . Um-mmmm. I listened and I heared him say, 'God don't wake up nobody's chilluns but his own.' Ummm-a . . . Ummm-a."

The prayer was long. It rose like a chant, growing more

and more fervent, more musical, an obligato to the throbbing drone that ebbed and flowed in the church. The members continued to busy themselves with their shoes. With bowed heads the women ran their hands under their skirts to remove stockings. The men unhooked their garters and rolled up the legs of long stovepipe drawers.

"Amen, brother, amen."

The brother with carrot-colored hair rose from his knees. Then the pans were moved from the aisles and began passing unseen beneath the bowed figures who faced each other in the rows of seats. Feet touched water. Then it was that the real storm broke.

"Hallelujah, church."

"Shout, sweet peoples, shout."

"H'mmmm. Whee-ee!"

An elderly brother, as powerfully built as a gorilla, shook off those who tried to hold him and fought his way into the aisle. With his pants and his dirt-colored underwear rolled above his knees, he began to dance a thudding, tribal dance, stamping the floor with his wet bare feet.

Well, I be John Brown, Dink told himself, if old Moon Dawson ain't shouting the second time. He been a powerful man in his day, that there Moon Dawson. Shouting two time in one afternoon is going *some*—old as he is. Rev'm Lissus asked him to help keep the singing warm, but here he gone and got hisself happy first thing. Hmph, them chilluns'll have to get religion best way they can.

Suddenly old Moon halted, dropped both arms to his sides, and raised his face to the ceiling. Tears were streaming down his face.

"Here I'm crying like a baby," he bellowed, "and don't

know what I'm crying about." That seemed to amuse him. Old Moon laughed at himself heartily. "Ain't this something, now. What-wha-wha! I told you I'd break it up. Crying like a baby and don't know what I'm crying about. Wha-wha-wha!"

The youngsters on the moaners' bench were mildly interested. They raised their faces—those who were awake—then bowed them again, looking at each other with guilty smiles.

On the pulpit Rev'm Lissus girded himself with a towel, knelt and began washing the feet of a fellow preacher. Two white policemen, assuring themselves that the aisles were theoretically open, came down from the packed balcony and stood in the rear of the church with caps on their heads. A prissy brown couple, elaborately dressed and far too refined for the noisy business around them, managed to squeeze into a bench near the front.

Old Moon Dawson had finished his shout but he wasn't ready to sit down yet. He continued to roam the aisles, slapping his hands, laughing when he felt like it, crying when he was tired of laughing, bellowing in a great voice when a thought struck him.

"I told you I'd break it up. Who made God—tell me that."

"Glory, Jesus. Glory!"

A woman jumped out of her seat and raced the length of the church. Somewhere water splashed. A pan flew into the air and a powerful female tumbled into the laps of those who sat beside her on the bench, tumbled into their laps then rolled off onto the floor. There she lay, kicking and screaming. A man got up, stood behind his stout wife and held her firmly around the waist to keep her from embarrassing him. Thus she could only fling out her arms and legs and protest with her voice that she was happy, supremely happy, so happy she could roll a mile in the mud. A pair of lithe coffee damsels went into a replica of Moon Dawson's barefoot dance, and Dink observed with a little surprise that there were now ten barefoot women in the aisles and three men. Things were really becoming intense. Even Dink was conscious of a quick, cool sensation, a fleeting chill followed by warmth and prickly heat—was it happiness? Lordy, was it really happiness?

Tell me how did you feel
When you come out the wilderness,
Come out the wilderness,
Come out the wilderness?
Tell me how did you feel
When you come out the wilderness
Leaning on the Lord?

I feels good a plenty, Dink told himself, but that ain't helping them seven young-uns to come through. All the singing and carrying on is good a heap and I likes it all, but them devilish chilluns is fixing to go to sleep again. Lordy, me, the devil sure is got the best of young folkses now-days. Bless me, the spirit is *moving* here today, moving fit to waller a mule—and look-a yonder at them kids. Lordy, help. Lordy, do, please . . .

Did yo' soul feel happy
When you come out the wilderness?

A tide of song . . . Waves surging and breaking . . . A storm of voices with winds rushing . . . A storm with thunder . . . Now and again the shock and flash of lightning.

"Glory be! I feels it. Hallelujah!"

Old Moon Dawson was still roaming the aisles, bellowing.

"You talk about the devil—well, where he come from? Who ever seen him? Wha-wha-wha! I told you I'd break it up."

Did you feel like shouting
When you come out the wilderness?

"Chilly water, church! I can't keep still."

Rev'm Lissus, his feet washed, slipped on his old socks and shoes and came down to the rail. He slapped his hands and raised them above his head. He opened his mouth and cried aloud to his Maker.

"Lord-Lord-Lord—Oh, Lord-Lord!"

Did you love eve'body?

"Pray, chillun," an old sister cried.

Come out the wilderness,
Come out the wilderness,
Come out the wilderness . . .

Then again there was that unseen bolt, that electrifying shock in the midst of the storm. It brought Dink up with a jerk that nearly wrenched his neck, and he saw that the children on the moaners' bench had opened their eyes abruptly and that their mouths were round with astonishment. A cry went up in the back of the church that was unlike any that had been heard before, a cry that one doesn't expect to hear outside the jungle, a cry that seemed a trifle less and a trifle more than human, a cry that one felt was somehow akin to witchery and to the animal kingdom at the same time. It didn't say *glory;* it didn't say *hallelujah,* and it didn't say *Jesus.* It simply screamed, and Dink's blood froze in his veins. What was it? Who? Lordy! Then suddenly he knew.

Dark, cat-like and mysterious, she rose from her bench near the rear, leaped to the back of the seat in the front of her, and began running along on the tops of the benches. Faster than the eye could follow, light of foot, almost ghost-like, she went from one bench-back to the next. Down about half way to the front, back to the rear, and then with a fresh burst of speed, the whole length of the church. Was it happiness? Lordy, Dink thought, was it really happiness? How long would it last? It was absurd to think of breathing before it was over. She approached the bench on which the seven children were "moaning." Now it was just one step ahead. But right here a miracle happened.

Perhaps, like Peter walking on the sea, her faith failed. Perhaps—but the cause is unimportant. The dark, shadowy woman lost her lightness quite as suddenly as she had gained it. Her feet lost the cat-like certainty. And when she touched the back of the children's bench, she touched it with the foot of a natural woman.

With a crash the bench toppled over. The children, scattered across the floor in front of the pulpit, screamed and cried with fright. The woman sprawled among them, exhausted and unconscious. Then gradually, bit by bit, a peculiar significance began to dawn on Dink, on Rev'm Lissus, on old Moon Dawson, and on all the women folks.

Dink didn't dare put the thought into words. He was still blinking, unable to believe his eyes. But, sure as life, there were the seven children rolling on the floor, kicking, screaming, and (undoubtedly) praising God.

"Hallelujah," Rev'm Lissus shouted. "Glory be—glory be!"

"Shout, sweet peoples. My chile is done got religion," a mother cried. "My chile is got happy and come through, praise Jesus."

"Mine, too, Jesus. Mine too."

One mother came running down the aisle and fell on the neck of the little fellow who had slept throughout most of the service.

"I'm so glad," she said. "Honey baby, yo' mammy is *so* glad." Then she began to wail as if she might presently get happy herself.

There was confusion without end in Mount Pleasant. Wave after wave rose and broke against the rafters. But nothing else mattered now. The children had got religion. The young-uns had got happy and come through, thanks the Lord. It was just too wonderful.

Dink didn't aim to shout himself. As a matter of fact, he didn't even feel it coming, but when he saw all them devilish chillun sprawled out before the altar, a-kicking and a-carrying on—well, it was just too much for a God-fearing man to stand up against. Dink lost control.

He must have done some powerful shouting, but he couldn't remember very definitely. When he came to, the church was nearly empty and he had the floors and the pans and the windows and such things to think about. He got a broom from behind the pulpit and tried to decide which end of the church needed his attention most urgently. He stooped down and squinted under the benches.

"Lordy, look a-there," he muttered. "Right where them kids was sitting, too." It was the debris of a roasted sweet potato. "Can you beat that?" he asked himself thoughtfully. "Whilst all us was a-praying and trying to pull them through, one of them brats took a sweet tater outta his pocket and eat it up clean. The devil sure is got the best of young-uns now-days. I be doggone if he ain't."

A SUMMER TRAGEDY

Old Jeff Patton, the black share farmer, fumbled with his bow tie. His fingers trembled, and the high, stiff collar pinched his throat. A fellow loses his hand for such vanities after thirty or forty years of simple life. Once a year, or maybe twice if there's a wedding among his kin-folks, he may spruce up; but generally fancy clothes do nothing but adorn the wall of the big room and feed the moths. That had been Jeff Patton's experience. He had not worn his stiff-bosomed shirt more than a dozen times in all his married life. His swallowtailed coat lay on the bed beside him, freshly brushed and pressed, but it was as full of holes as the overalls in which he worked on week days. The moths had used it badly. Jeff twisted his mouth into a hideous toothless grimace as he contended with the obstinate bow. He stamped his good foot and decided to give up the struggle.

"Jennie," he called.

"What's that, Jeff?" His wife's shrunken voice came out

of the adjoining room like an echo. It was hardly bigger than a whisper.

"I reckon you'll have to he'p me wid this heah bow tie, baby," he said meekly. "Dog if I can hitch it up."

Her answer was not strong enough to reach him, but presently the old woman came to the door, feeling her way with a stick. She had a wasted, dead-leaf appearance. Her body, as scrawny and gnarled as a stringbean, seemed less than nothing in the ocean of frayed and faded petticoats that surrounded her. These hung an inch or two above the tops of her heavy, unlaced shoes and showed little grotesque piles where the stockings had fallen down from her negligible legs.

"You oughta could do a heap mo' wid a thing like that 'n me—beingst as you got yo' good sight."

"Looks like I *oughta* could," he admitted. "But ma fingers is gone democrat on me. I get all mixed up in the looking glass an' can't tell whicha way to twist the devilish thing."

Jennie sat on the side of the bed and old Jeff Patton got down on one knee while she tied the bow knot. It was a slow and painful ordeal for each of them in this position. Jeff's bones cracked, his knee ached, and it was only after a half dozen attempts that Jennie worked a semblance of a bow into the tie.

"I got to dress maself now," the old woman whispered. "These is ma old shoes an' stockings, and I ain't so much as unwrapped ma dress."

"Well, don't worry 'bout me no mo', baby," Jeff said. "That 'bout finishes me. All I gotta do now is slip on that old coat 'n ves' an' I'll be fixed to leave."

Jennie disappeared again through the dim passage into the shed room. Being blind was no handicap to her in that black hole. Jeff heard the cane placed against the wall beside the door and knew that his wife was on easy ground. He put on his coat, took a battered top hat from the bed post, and hobbled to the front door. He was ready to travel. As soon as Jennie could get on her Sunday shoes and her old black silk dress, they would start.

Outside the tiny log house the day was warm and mellow with sunshine. A host of wasps was humming with busy excitement in the trunk of a dead sycamore. Grey squirrels were searching through the grass for hickory nuts and blue jays were in the trees, hopping from branch to branch. Pine woods stretched away to the left like a black sea. Among them were scattered scores of log houses like Jeff's, houses of black share farmers. Cows and pigs wandered freely among the trees. There was no danger of loss. Each farmer knew his own stock and knew his neighbor's as well as he knew his neighbor's children.

Down the slope to the right were the cultivated acres on which the colored folks worked. They extended to the river, more than two miles away, and they were today green with the unmade cotton crop. A tiny thread of a road, which passed directly in front of Jeff's place, ran through these green fields like a pencil mark.

Jeff, standing outside the door with his absurd hat in his left hand, surveyed the wide scene tenderly. He had been forty-five years on these acres. He loved them with the unexplained affection that others have for the countries to which they belong.

The sun was hot on his head, his collar still pinched his

throat, and the Sunday clothes were intolerably hot. Jeff transferred the hat to his right hand and began fanning with it. Suddenly the whisper that was Jennie's voice came out of the shed room.

"You can bring the car round front whilst you's waitin'," it said feebly. There was a tired pause; then it added, "I'll soon be fixed to go."

"A'right, baby," Jeff answered. "I'll get it in a minute."

But he didn't move. A thought struck him that made his mouth fall open. The mention of the car brought to his mind, with new intensity, the trip he and Jennie were about to take. Fear came into his eyes; excitement took his breath. Lord, Jesus!

"Jeff . . . Oh Jeff," the old woman's whisper called.

He awakened with a jolt. "Hunh, baby?"

"What you doin'?"

"Nuthin. Jes studyin'. I jes been turnin' things round 'n round in ma mind."

"You could be gettin' the car," she said.

"Oh yes, right away, baby."

He started round to the shed, limping heavily on his bad leg. There were three frizzly chickens in the yard. All his other chickens had been killed or stolen recently. But the frizzly chickens had been saved somehow. That was fortunate indeed, for these curious creatures had a way of devouring "poison" from the yard and in that way protecting against conjure and bad luck and spells. But even the frizzly chickens seemed now to be in a stupor. Jeff thought they had some ailment; he expected all three of them to die shortly.

The shed in which the old model-T Ford stood was only

a grass roof held up by four corner poles. It had been built by tremulous hands at a time when the little rattle-trap car had been regarded as a peculiar treasure. And, miraculously, despite wind and downpour, it still stood.

Jeff adjusted the crank and put his weight on it. The engine came to life with a sputter and bang that rattled the old car from radiator to tail light. Jeff hopped into the seat and put his foot on the accelerator. The sputtering and banging increased. The rattling became more violent. That was good. It was good banging, good sputtering and rattling, and it meant that the aged car was still in running condition. She could be depended on for this trip.

Again Jeff's thought halted as if paralyzed. The suggestion of the trip fell into the machinery of his mind like a wrench. He felt dazed and weak. He swung the car out into the yard, made a half turn, and drove around to the front door. When he took his hands off the wheel, he noticed that he was trembling violently. He cut off the motor and climbed to the ground to wait for Jennie.

A few moments later she was at the window, her voice rattling against the pane like a broken shutter.

"I'm ready, Jeff."

He did not answer, but limped into the house and took her by the arm. He led her slowly through the big room, down the step, and across the yard.

"You reckon I'd oughta lock the do'?" he asked softly.

They stopped and Jennie weighed the question. Finally she shook her head.

"Ne' mind the do'," she said. "I don't see no cause to lock up things."

"You right," Jeff agreed. "No cause to lock up."

Jeff opened the door and helped his wife into the car. A quick shudder passed over him. Jesus! Again he trembled.

"How come you shaking so?" Jennie whispered.

"I don't know," he said.

"You mus' be scairt, Jeff."

"No, baby, I ain't scairt."

He slammed the door after her and went around to crank up again. The motor started easily. Jeff wished that it had not been so responsive. He would have liked a few more minutes in which to turn things around in his head. As it was, with Jennie chiding him about being afraid, he had to keep going. He swung the car into the little pencil-mark road and started off toward the river, driving very slowly, very cautiously.

Chugging across the green countryside, the small, battered Ford seemed tiny indeed. Jeff felt a familiar excitement, a thrill, as they came down the first slope to the immense levels on which the cotton was growing. He could not help reflecting that the crops were good. He knew what that meant, too; he had made forty-five of them with his own hands. It was true that he had worn out nearly a dozen mules, but that was the fault of old man Stevenson, the owner of the land. Major Stevenson had the odd notion that one mule was all a share farmer needed to work a thirty-acre plot. It was an expensive notion, the way it killed mules from overwork, but the old man held to it. Jeff thought it killed a good many share farmers as well as mules, but he had no sympathy for them. He had always been strong, and he had been taught to have no patience with weakness in men. Women or children might be tolerated if they were puny, but a weak man was a curse. Of course, his own children—

Jeff's thought halted there. He and Jennie never mentioned their dead children any more. And naturally he did not wish to dwell upon them in his mind. Before he knew it, some remark would slip out of his mouth and that would make Jennie feel blue. Perhaps she would cry. A woman like Jennie could not easily throw off the grief that comes from losing five grown children within two years. Even Jeff was still staggered by the blow. His memory had not been much good recently. He frequently talked to himself. And, although he had kept it a secret, he knew that his courage had left him. He was terrified by the least unfamiliar sound at night. He was reluctant to venture far from home in the daytime. And that habit of trembling when he felt fearful was now far beyond his control. Sometimes he became afraid and trembled without knowing what had frightened him. The feeling would just come over him like a chill.

The car rattled slowly over the dusty road. Jennie sat erect and silent, with a little absurd hat pinned to her hair. Her useless eyes seemed very large and very white in their deep sockets. Suddenly Jeff heard her voice, and he inclined his head to catch the words.

"Is we passed Delia Moore's house yet?" she asked.

"Not yet," he said.

"You must be drivin' mighty slow, Jeff."

"We jes as well take our time, baby."

There was a pause. A little puff of steam was coming out of the radiator of the car. Heat wavered above the hood. Delia Moore's house was nearly half a mile away. After a moment Jennie spoke again.

"You ain't really scairt, is you, Jeff?"

"Nah, baby, I ain't scairt."

"You know how we agreed–we gotta keep on goin'."

Jewels of perspiration appeared on Jeff's forehead. His eyes rounded, blinked, became fixed on the road.

"I don't know," he said with a shiver. "I reckon it's the only thing to do."

"Hm."

A flock of guinea fowls, pecking in the road, were scattered by the passing car. Some of them took to their wings; others hid under bushes. A blue jay, swaying on a leafy twig, was annoying a roadside squirrel. Jeff held an even speed till he came near Delia's place. Then he slowed down noticeably.

Delia's house was really no house at all, but an abandoned store building converted into a dwelling. It sat near a crossroads, beneath a single black cedar tree. There Delia, a catlike old creature of Jennie's age, lived alone. She had been there more years than anybody could remember, and long ago had won the disfavor of such women as Jennie. For in her young days Delia had been gayer, yellower, and saucier than seemed proper in those parts. Her ways with menfolks had been dark and suspicious. And the fact that she had had as many husbands as children did not help her reputation.

"Yonder's old Delia," Jeff said as they passed.

"What she doin'?"

"Jes sittin' in the do'," he said.

"She see us?"

"Hm," Jeff said. "Musta did."

That relieved Jennie. It strengthened her to know that her old enemy had seen her pass in her best clothes. That would give the old she-devil something to chew her gums and fret about, Jennie thought. Wouldn't she have a fit if she didn't find out? Old evil Delia! This would be just the thing for her. It would pay her back for being so evil. It would also pay her, Jennie thought, for the way she used to grin at Jeff—long ago when her teeth were good.

The road became smooth and red, and Jeff could tell by the smell of the air that they were nearing the river. He could see the rise where the road turned and ran along parallel to the stream. The car chugged on monotonously. After a long silent spell, Jennie leaned against Jeff and spoke.

"How many bale o' cotton you think we got standin'?" she said.

Jeff wrinkled his forehead as he calculated.

" 'Bout twenty-five, I reckon."

"How many you make las' year?"

"Twenty-eight," he said. "How come you ask that?"

"I's jes thinkin'," Jennie said quietly.

"It don't make a speck o' diff'ence though," Jeff reflected. "If we get much or if we get little, we still gonna be in debt to old man Stevenson when he gets through counting up agin us. It's took us a long time to learn that."

Jennie was not listening to these words. She had fallen into a trance-like meditation. Her lips twitched. She chewed her gums and rubbed her old gnarled hands nervously. Suddenly, she leaned forward, buried her face in the nervous hands, and burst into tears. She cried aloud in a dry, cracked voice that suggested the rattle of fodder on dead stalks. She cried aloud like a child, for she had never learned to suppress a genuine sob. Her slight old frame shook heavily and seemed hardly able to sustain such violent grief.

"What's the matter, baby?" Jeff asked awkwardly. "Why you cryin' like all that?"

"I's jes thinkin'," she said.

"So you the one what's scairt now, hunh?"

"I ain't scairt, Jeff. I's jes thinkin' 'bout leavin' eve'thing like this—eve'thing we been used to. It's right sad-like."

Jeff did not answer, and presently Jennie buried her face again and continued crying.

The sun was almost overhead. It beat down furiously on the dusty wagon path road, on the parched roadside grass, and the tiny battered car. Jeff's hands, gripping the wheel, became wet with perspiration; his forehead sparkled. Jeff's lips parted and his mouth shaped a hideous grimace. His face suggested the face of a man being burned. But the torture passed and his expression softened again.

"You mustn't cry, baby," he said to his wife. "We gotta be strong. We can't break down."

Jennie waited a few seconds, then said, "You reckon we oughta do it, Jeff? You reckon we oughta go 'head an' do it really?"

Jeff's voice choked; his eyes blurred. He was terrified to hear Jennie say the thing that had been in his mind all morning. She had egged him on when he had wanted more than anything in the world to wait, to reconsider, to think things over a little longer. Now *she* was getting cold feet.

Actually, there was no need of thinking the question through again. It would only end in making the same painful decision once more. Jeff knew that. There was no need of fooling around longer.

"We jes as well to do like we planned," he said. "They ain't nuthin else for us now—it's the bes' thing."

Jeff thought of the handicaps, the near impossibility, of making another crop with his leg bothering him more and more each week. Then there was always the chance that he would have another stroke, like the one that had made him lame. Another one might kill him. The least it could do would be to leave him helpless. Jeff gasped . . . Lord, Jesus! He could not bear to think of being helpless, like a baby, on Jennie's hands. Frail, blind Jennie.

The little pounding motor of the car worked harder and harder. The puff of steam from the cracked radiator became larger. Jeff realized that they were climbing a little rise. A moment later the road turned abruptly and he looked down upon the face of the river.

"Jeff."

"Hunh?"

"Is that the water I hear?"

"Hm. Tha's it."

"Well, which way you goin' now?"

"Down this-a way," he answered. "The road runs 'long-side o' the water a lil piece."

She waited a while calmly. Then she said, "Drive faster."

"A'right, baby," Jeff said.

The water roared in the bed of the river. It was fifty or sixty feet below the level of the road. Between the road and the water there was a long smooth slope, sharply inclined. The slope was dry; the clay had been hardened by prolonged summer heat. The water below, roaring in a narrow channel, was noisy and wild.

"Jeff."

"Hunh?"

"How far you goin'?"

"Jes a lil piece down the road."

"You ain't scairt is you, Jeff?"

"Nah, baby," he said trembling. "I ain't scairt."

"Remember how we planned it, Jeff. We gotta do it like we said. Brave-like."

"Hm."

Jeff's brain darkened. Things suddenly seemed unreal, like figures in a dream. Thoughts swam in his mind foolishly, hysterically, like little blind fish in a pool within a dense cave. They rushed, crossed one another, jostled, collided, retreated, and rushed again. Jeff soon became dizzy. He shuddered violently and turned to his wife.

"Jennie, I can't do it. I can't." His voice broke pitifully.

She did not appear to be listening. All the grief had gone from her face. She sat erect, her unseeing eyes wide open, strained and frightful. Her glossy black skin had become dull. She seemed as thin and as sharp and bony as a starved bird. Now, having suffered and endured the sadness of tearing herself away from beloved things, she showed no anguish. She was absorbed with her own thoughts, and she didn't even hear Jeff's voice shouting in her ear.

Jeff said nothing more. For an instant there was light in

his cavernous brain. That chamber was, for less than a second, peopled by characters he knew and loved. They were simple, healthy creatures, and they behaved in a manner that he could understand. They had quality. But since he had already taken leave of them long ago, the remembrance did not break his heart again. Young Jeff Patton was among them, the Jeff Patton of fifty years ago who went down to New Orleans with a crowd of country boys to the Mardi Gras doings. The gay young crowd—boys with candy-striped shirts and rouged brown girls in noisy silks—was like a picture in his head. Yet it did not make him sad. On that very trip Slim Burns had killed Joe Beasley—the crowd had been broken up. Since then Jeff Patton's world had been the Greenbrier Plantation. If there had been other Mardi Gras carnivals, he had not heard of them. Since then there had been no time; the years had fallen on him like waves. Now he was old, worn out. Another paralytic stroke like the one he had already suffered would put him on his back for keeps. In that condition, with a frail blind woman to look after him, he would be worse off than if he were dead.

Suddenly Jeff's hands became steady. He actually felt brave. He slowed down the motor of the car and carefully pulled off the road. Below, the water of the stream boomed, a soft thunder in the deep channel. Jeff ran the car onto the clay slope, pointed it directly toward the stream, and put his foot heavily on the accelerator. The little car leaped furiously down the steep incline toward the water. The movement was nearly as swift and direct as a fall. The two old black folks, sitting quietly side by side, showed no excitement. In another instant the car hit the water and dropped immediately out of sight.

A little later it lodged in the mud of a shallow place. One wheel of the crushed and upturned little Ford became visible above the rushing water.

HOPPERGRASS MAN

The black boy called Ski—the skinny one with the unbelievable feet—put his shoulder blades against a telegraph pole, crossed his legs, and spat neatly through the gap in his upper front teeth.

Come to think about it, why shouldn't he put on a little dog? Wasn't Sunday the day for sporting? Wasn't he wearing a brand new pink shirt under his overall jumper? The devil with all that long-faced, down-in-the-heels mess! Ski believed in having his fun when Sunday came. His mouth was nearly dry by now, but he worked his jaws hard and finally produced enough saliva to send another thin white spout into the dusty road. Ski knew that he was a devil-raising sort of somebody—spitting like all that, crossing his legs, and carrying on the way he did on a Sunday afternoon—and right now he was glad of it. There were women folk on the path.

They came from Mr. Tom Tucker's place beyond the branch, followed the barbed wire fence across the low field, disappeared in a thicket of wild plum, and then emerged on the narrow foot way that ran into the big road.

They were all carrying hickory switches, and Ski concluded that they were going fishing. He listened to the blur of voices and strained his eyes to make out the faces that flashed now and again between the green clumps. Yes, the two in front were Varee and Doll. That short one was Mousie. The other two—well, it didn't make a heap of difference to Ski who the other two were, so long as neither one was Susy. And from this distance he felt quite sure that nobody in the crowd was half big enough to be Susy Maud. He rubbed his back against the pole, scratching a spot that had commenced to itch, and began working his jaws again. He'd need a powerful lot of saliva in his mouth to impress that crowd of hinky brown gals with his spitting. Yes, suh, them gals from the Tucker place all chewed 'baccer themselves. H'm, they knowed what sure 'nough spitting was. Ski did not underestimate them.

"What's on yo' mind, Ski-feets?"

There they were already. Ski grinned broadly, fixed his mouth, and spat handsomely through the gap in his teeth. He wasn't looking directly at the crowd of young women but he heard them twitter as his tongue clicked against his teeth. His chest began to swell.

"What y'-all gals giggling about?" he said devilishly. "You must be noticed my brand new pink silk shirt what I got on."

"Humph!" a heavy female voice said. *"Humph!"*

Ski raised his eyes, his mouth dropping open. There, sure enough, as big as life and as ugly, he saw the huge figure of Susy Maud looming up behind Varee and Doll and Mouse and Lou. Was it recognition that put the bright spot in her eye? And him—Lordy, what a plague-gone fool he was not to see a woman as big and black as Susy Maud. And her standing right there in front of him all the time! Having the shirt on wasn't insult enough. No, like a monkey he had to open his mouth and talk about it in the woman's very presence.

Susy's big voice, her broad shoulders, and her powerful arms put gooseflesh on Ski. Her grunts silenced the other women as well. Ski wondered if she were accusing him, secretly, as she set her arms akimbo, boring holes in him with her eyes. Did Susy Maud really suspect him?

Of course, Ski hadn't exactly stolen the shirt. It had simply fallen into his hands. A week earlier, when he had driven a group to town on Saturday night, someone had left a parcel in his wagon. The thing turned out to be this gaudy shirt, and evidence at once pointed to Susy Maud as its owner. But Ski had coveted the bright thing from the first, and that was why he had schemed to own it.

It was impossible to know whether Susy, in buying the shirt, had mistaken it for a woman's shirtwaist or whether she had intended to make a present of it to some unrevealed "gentaman" friend. And it was actually no matter now. Ski got his hands on it and laid his plans carefully. After a night of plotting he decided on a course of action. The next day he met Susy in the door of the church, holding the garment unwrapped before her while all the folks looked on.

"This here yo' shirt, Susy Maud?" he said with a leer. There was heavy ridicule on his words. "I found it in my wagon when y'-all gals got out last night. It must be b'longs to some of you. He-he-he! Some of y'-all must be got a sweet man you's dressing up. He-he-he! This a stomping down pretty shirt, for a fact."

Susy Maud had appeared to be on the verge of snatching the thing from his hand, but at the same moment she had noticed the preacher standing behind her on the church steps. She had regained her society manners in time to laugh it off.

"You's a crying mess, old Ski-feets. What in the nation you 'spect I'm doing with a gentaman's pink silk shirt? You better go 'way from me, boy."

But as she said it her little eyes flashed, and Ski knew that the experience had rankled in her bosom.

This afternoon, meeting the skinny, big-foot boy on the roadside, she exploded. Ski looked at her intently, his lips feeling suddenly parched, and waited for the crisis.

"Listen," she said, pushing the other girls aside with her elbows. "You ain't smart-talking nobody, Ski-feets—on'erstand?"

"Who, me? You talking 'bout me, Susy Maud?"

"I got me a good mind to—"

She made a gesture with the long hickory switch.

"Mind out, now, you better stay in yo' place, Susy Maud."

The other four girls giggled and withdrew. Ski saw them in the middle of the road a moment later. They were standing with hands on their hips, lips apart, teeth flashing.

In the same instant Susy Maud drew back and gave him a lash on the arm. Then she told him what it was for.

"Mind out how you takes things what don't belong to you—hear?"

"Woman–" Ski rolled his eyes bitterly.

"Don't you say a word to me," Susy Maud cried. "I'm gonna woman you–you frog-eyed varmint."

He felt himself lashed twice. He opened his mouth to speak but lost his breath when she reached him a third time, with a cruel cut across the face.

"You gonna make me mad, Susy. I'm apt to forget you's a woman directly."

"Hush," she told him between swipes. "Hush, I says. You might well forget I's a woman but I bound you, you won't forget what I'm gonna put on yo' back before I quits."

She settled down to the work in deep earnest, dug her toes into the ground, and began putting one hundred and ninety pounds into each swing. Ski looked at her through round, baffled eyes. He knew he couldn't stand there forever catching such heavy punishment, but what was he to do? Susy Maud had lost her mind. She wouldn't pay attention to anything he said. Lordy–that *was* a terrible lick.

"You's got good aim," he told her softly.

"Think so?"

"Mighty right, I do. But you draws back too far. I could just–"

Ski raised his hand to strike her, but promptly caught a lash over the head for his gesture. He decided not to try that again.

"What was you 'bout to say just now, Ski?"

He did not answer. The surrounding fields were quiet, vibrant and mournful in the late afternoon. Between Susy Maud's well-timed swipes Ski could hear the drone of insects in a roadside thicket. A July-fly set up a giddy hum in the top of a scrubby pine tree. Ski kept assuring himself that he couldn't continue to stand there with Susy Maud getting stronger and stronger on the end of her hickory switch.

Presently, he made a decision. The girls were still giggling in the road, but Ski didn't care if they did laugh now. He wasn't going to let big old blue-gummed Susy Maud beat him to death—leastwise, not while he still had his good feet and legs. He turned quickly and started across the field.

"H'm," he murmured, running hard. "Good thing I thought 'bout this. Susy Maud must be aimed to kill me in cold blood. That big old blue-gummed woman must be aimed to beat me to death right there on the spot, front of them other gals. H'm—"

Then, without warning, all the breath went out of him. A sidearm swipe caught him under the ribs and came within a eyelash of starching Ski. He halted, panting, bowing low and struggling to regain his strength. But Susy Maud gave him no rest. She had outrun his first dash, and now she began punishing him again, her feet digging solidly into the ground, her breath released in little explosive grunts with each swing.

Dazed, ready to fall after every stride, he made his way toward the big mule barn of Mr. Bob Leslie. Susy Maud beat him all the way. She whipped him in every downstairs part of the barn, in every mule stall, and she followed him up the ladder to the hayloft. There Ski's eyes fell upon a hayfork; but when he started toward it, he found his way barred by Susy and he was instantly sorry he had betrayed his real desperation. But the break only increased the woman's bitterness.

In time her glance ran to the door swinging open at the end of the loft. There was a frame of clear blue, a deep expanse like a sea, and outside a drop of fifteen or twenty feet to the ground. Susy Maud's gaze fixed on this opening as she backed Ski blindly toward the opening, pouring the hot lashes on his arms, across his head, down his back. Then suddenly the black boy's eyes opened as if he had just awakened from sleep.

"Jump," Susy Maud shouted. "Jump, you hoppergrass, you!"

Lordy, there he was at the jumping place for true. The huge woman blazed at him with fiery eyes. She meant business, this old blue-gummed Susy, and Ski knew it well and good. Lordy, was she getting ready to leap at him? He threw his arms up in terror and reached out desperately.

To his own surprise he laid hands on something he could hold.

Thanks the Lord, he thought. Please you, suh, I means to hold fast from here on. I means to hold faster and mo' fast, if that's what it takes.

His arms tightened. Yes, he saw it was Susy. He was groggy, but he had taken a firm grip while her arms were raised, and while he held them above her head in that way, she was unable to put the same force into her licks. She puffed and squirmed vigorously, but Ski held fast. One glimpse at the drop beyond the loft door put renewed strength into his arms.

Suddenly, and quite to his comfort, he observed that the blows were becoming even lighter. Was Susy played out and tired—big old powerful Susy Maud? Had she changed her mind? How come she just tapped him easy-like now?

Ski didn't bother to answer. In this astounding manner, his mind buzzing with questions, his body bruised and aching, Ski found love.

"You old no-'count hoppergrass man, you," he heard her saying in a changed voice.

"You big old ugly kettle of chitterlings," he answered, touched.

"Devilish hound-dog, you." It was spoken fondly.

Ski averted his face and spat neatly, between the gap in his upper front teeth, against the wall.

"You old greasy faced, sop-the-plate sweet potato."

Love softened the blows and finished them. Twilight came to the hayloft with mauve shadows. The two dark figures clasped each other with powerful arms, trembling.

"What 'bout this pretty shirt of yo's?" Ski said.

"Keep it," she answered. "It's *yo's*. I bought it for you from the first, you ign'ant hoppergrass, you."

SATURDAY NIGHT

Portrait of a Small Southern Town, 1933

Day ends abruptly here. The Alabama twilight is as brief and lovely as a rainbow. A host of excited chimney-swifts leave the broken flues of a ruined old mansion, waver upward, fleck the mauve sky for an instant, then disappear.

Suddenly we become aware of wagons—mule carts—on the red-dirt county road. In one there is a family of black share farmers; four girls, three boys, and the old couple. The girls and the woman wear blood-red dresses made of identical cloth; and the boys, under their overall straps, have on blouses cut from the same tawdry bolt. The wizened old father has on a shirt of a suspiciously similar complexion, but fortunately it is pretty well covered by his overall jumper. All the faces are as round as full moons. At the moment they wear smiles. In another wagon a smaller family of poor whites rides behind a team of leaner mules. Two men sit in the front seat with necks thrust out, their cheeks bulging with tobacco. There is an old woman and a young one in the second seat, and a small boy on the floor. These folks have things to sell: a coop of half-grown chickens, several bushels of sweet potatoes, some green vegetables. And there is a bundle of fodder for the restless, waiting team when it reaches the square in the heart of town. Other wagons follow.

In passing our gate not one of them fails to pause long enough to notice the license plates on the battered Chevrolet in the driveway. Thanks to the Scottsboro case and the reports of more recent Communistic activities here, all New Yorkers, black or white, are held in suspicion—this in addition to the traditional distrust of strangers. We wave our arms from the doorsteps.

"Good evening."

"H'm. 'Evenin', p'fesser. 'Evenin'."

It is hard to explain the title they have given me so confidently on first sight. Maybe it is because I am dressed too well for a share farmer and too poorly for a rural doctor.

A few moments later we are in the procession, our light car leaping joyously on the sorry road. It does not occur to us till we turn onto the paved pike that none of the wagons carry lanterns. When we are driving at forty or better, they materialize like ghosts out of the darkness and we are obliged to slam on brakes and skid for our lives. It is the same with the people walking on the pavement; they never step off the concrete to favor a passing automobile. We drop down to twenty and comment bitterly on this attitude. Some night a reckless young fellow, momentarily blinded perhaps by the lights of an approaching car, is going to pick one of them off. Before reaching the city limits we have occasion to swerve perilously in order to miss a wandering cow, and at another point we stop dead still while a small herd of goats crosses the pike. Another brief spurt and we come into the aged little town. Where shall we go now?

In New York or Chicago we would never ask that question. There one leaves home with a fixed purpose, accomplishes it, and returns. The going is incidental to the objective. Here the going is the thing. Whatever one does, the romance of the journey is unpremeditated. One does not even decide what groceries he will buy on a Saturday night. Since we *shall* buy, however, and since the principal stores face the courthouse square, it might be well to begin there.

The white stone building with its wide austere steps on four sides sits on a green knoll, surrounded by giant oaks. On the grassy slopes there are the usual cannon mounted. Apparently the Confederacy has never disarmed; the South, the stranger gathers, is still in rebellion. Was it H. L. Mencken who first made this observation? It is charmingly true. On the steps of one side a political stump speaker is in action; he is seeking a petty office in the county. He has drawn a strictly riffraff crowd by his strident oratory.

". . . Take Macon County fer'n instance. Down yonder there's seven niggers to every white man. Why, if anything was to happen . . . Yet 'n still they got heap better roads 'n we got here in Madison County."

A swarm of hucksters surrounds the square. A few of them have forsaken their carts to join the crowd on the steps, but the larger number are not interested. It does not disturb them that there are seven niggers to one white man in Macon County; they know that there are less than seven customers, black or white, to one huckster in Madison County, and that is the real issue. It is a tribute to these that now, even in this county, a man is not certain to be swept into office on the rebound of such a speech.

A picturesque old editor in a black frock coat, with flowing silver hair, a cane, a ten-gallon hat, and a mysterious reputation, pauses a moment to re-light his cigar and to catch a few words from the speaker. We are told that before the war this editor owned and published the town's first string newspaper. Then something happened, something. . . . Now he is publishing a rival paper. He is the only man we have seen who *looks* Southern, and he manifests a melodramatic interest in the story of the seven niggers to one white man. It is easy to believe that the genesis of racial antagonism is with just such men—petty politicians, rural editors, and their like. The poor whites have taken too much blame. The white peasantry and the black are at peace except when harried and driven by these.

Gradually the streets have become crowded, but everyone seems to be idle, soberly gawking into shop windows to pass the time. In the next block we learn that the local Ford agency has gone out of business—"after all these years." That is the first vivid mark of the depression we discover. Somehow it is hard to realize that Fords are not selling. No wonder the rustics in overalls gawk into lighted windows, no wonder there is pain and defeat on their faces. No wonder the town is sick.

* * *

We wander from shop to shop, buying apples and popcorn balls and hamburgers, but the horror of that comparison stays with us, and we know in our hearts that we have touched the nerve of this town's sore. Medievalism. Medieval serfs. Medieval lords. Medieval poverty. Medieval religion. Medieval thoughts. Medieval woes. There is no modern doubt here, no robust skepticism. This town takes its traditions without a quibble. It has never stopped to question its axioms, its institutions, its prejudices, its politics. Medieval credulity. And hence, in this black time, it has now accepted defeat. The peasants gawk stupidly into shop windows.

Fortunately, the earth is good. There are bushel baskets on the cobblestones, overflowing with fine potatoes. Corn is too cheap to sell. The small farmers are keeping theirs for home use. Green vegetables abound. There is no want of food.

Fortunately, too (prohibition to the contrary), there are still ways in which a poor man may brace his courage and make brave gestures. Old Badfoot Tyson is a case. A solitary, eccentric farmer, he had a decent crop of watermelons last summer. But Badfoot made the mistake of planting his melons too near the road. They were discovered by the boys of one of the colored schools. They made away with most of the crop, and the little game-legged man swore bitterly. One day a few weeks later when he was in the Negro barber shop getting a bottle of the particular hair tonic he had learned to drink, he heard that a crowd of students from the colored school had gone up the pike on a truck for a day's outing. This information evidently remained in his thought even after he had emptied the bottle of "hair tonic," for he went home, got his double-barreled shotgun, and started up the road. He found a jutting rock that hung over a high embankment and sat there to await the return of the students. Then when the truck did return, as it reached the turn where Badfoot was perched on the overhanging rock, he raised his gun, leveled it, and cut loose with both barrels. Half a dozen youngsters were swept from the flat bed of the truck. The old half-witted and drunken farmer cackled hoarsely and tumbled into the weeds below the embankment.

Our groceries bought, we drift over to the Negro street where our car is parked. The chauffeur of a local millionaire family, who looks enough like Paul Robeson to be his twin brother, flashes his Packard into the block, stops before the pool hall, and gets out leisurely. There is no gawking or despair in this block. It is true that Cynthe, the professional beggar woman, is a medievalism, but the depression has plainly hurt these folks but little. They have never had plenty; and want is only a trifle sharper than before. On the other hand the big men of the town have been softened. The business houses are especially kind.

We walk very slowly. In the Italian market there is a beautiful display of fresh red fish. In another place there is a pyramid of Florida oranges. The Negroes are all indolently ambling along. A little troop of backwoods musicians has stopped at the lunch counter. We can hear their guitars, their voices.

Back that train an' git yo'
Heavy load, O Lawdy;

SATURDAY NIGHT

Back that train an' git yo'
Heavy load.

Suddenly a black boy hurries by, consternation on his face. He enters the colored drug store. Presently, folks begin leaving the place. There is no indolence or ambling now. The Negroes walk rapidly. One, in his excitement, cuts across the street in the middle of the block. Another breaks into a run. All of them are getting off the main street, trying to make it to the darkened side-streets. A crowd starts pouring out of the pool hall. Men slip along the fronts of the buildings like shadows. We hear a whip pop; wagon wheels grind on the cobble stones.

What's up? What's it all about? Just a minute; tell me.

The best we get is a wild side glance. Terror is on the street. Out of the starry evening a warning has gone forth, something as tacit and ominous perhaps as the evidence that told Chicken Little the sky was falling. The result (on a more heroic scale) is the same. Not an audible word is spoken on the sidewalks—just the mute communication of animal to animal, then terror and flight. And while they scurry feverishly, we stand beneath the yellow blossom of the swaying street lamp and gesture vainly with our hands. Still they pass. The disdain, the utter scorn they have for us as outsiders is clearly manifest now. We are jostled roughly by a fat blubbery fellow whose breath we hear wheezing between his teeth, and when he turns to beg pardon, I take his arm firmly. The two of us plant our heels and shake our fingers in his face.

"You've got to tell us. We don't know what to do."

His eyes seem as round and flat as silver dollars. But

he perceives our earnestness and submits to the inquisition.

"A white man been kilt on the pike jes outa town."

"Murdered?"

"Nah, run over. Somebody hit him wid a car."

We cannot hide the fact that the news is less stirring than we had expected, and we are more perplexed than ever.

"Well. What about it?"

"They don't know who kilt him. That's what. The car ain't stopped."

The town's motorcycle cop, a short barrel-chested fellow with baby cheeks, a cigar dangling from his mouth, and a gun hanging from his belt, pops his motor, swings around the corner where we are standing, and dashes out toward the pike. A moment later an automobile careens dangerously on the same turn. There are two young men hanging on the running board. We restrain our prisoner with difficulty.

"Well . . ."

"It might o' been a cullud man what did that killin."

"Oh."

The light breaks. We know right well that it *was* a colored man who was driving that car. The others know it instinctively. We had to be told enough to put our minds on the right track. That driver refused to stop because he feared a mob.

The suave nut-brown pharmacist stands in the door of his place with hands thrust nervously into the pockets of his freshly laundered white coat. We go inside, order sodas, and sit down with him at one of the little round tables. All of us try hard to show ourselves unshaken by the panic on the streets. The druggist tells us that he studied at the Meharry Medical school in Nashville. We are glad to know him.

We can hear the sharp deliberate ticks of a small clock on a shelf. Presently the streets are empty.

Saturday night again—and again things to buy. The clerk in the chain store offers to bring our box of groceries out to the curb. *Hurry back!* We need meat, perhaps veal. . . . A few years ago in certain small towns of the South colored folks could not buy veal. The limited supply was frankly reserved for white customers. That seems far away; here we even have the effrontery to be exceedingly critical of that which is offered us.

On again; more shops, more purchases. The short bald man in the Jewish variety store stands against the glass door with hands in his pockets. He wears a dark sweater coat. The two or three Jews in this town are strangely unpleasant to Negroes. The blacks hold no malice, however. They feel that they understand. Even the illiterate blacks imagine they comprehend the psychological subtleties of race prejudice. They are amused by its vagaries. And in this one matter, we actually believe, the gods have in fun blessed them with an Olympian viewpoint.

But we have not forgotten the breathless pandemonium that filled these streets on the night of our last visit to town. Apparently the incident is forgotten. The huge good-looking chauffeur is standing beside his glistening Packard, a cigar held elegantly between his long fingers. Cynthe is on the street again, a snuff brush hanging from her lips, and her hand cupped in an attitude of medieval humility as she asks for a coin. The motor cop, cruising the streets leisurely, wears a big smile. Somehow we can't accept this tranquility. It is not natural that a night so charged with peril and drama should pass so lightly. Perhaps we need to adjust ourselves. There is a peculiar nervous preparation that we do not have, a certain diffidence. These black folks live on the very edges of a crater, and the grave danger that stops our breath merely to observe has ceased to terrify them. And we can see now that the excitement that drove them from the streets a week ago was no more than a good rain would have caused. They are neither tired nor depressed after that vigorous drain on their emotions.

The barber shop is crowded. The air is heavy with smoke and rustic political comment. Still we are unable to get an answer when we ask about the accident on the road. The decision of the Supreme Court in favor of a new trial for the Scottsboro boys still creates a lively stir, however. The black middle-aged barber, who seems to have a genius for catching the consensus of opinion, makes a whispered summary when the others have become quiet.

"The Alabama co't is gonna kill them boys for meanness now. You can bet yo' bottom dollar on that. Either they is gonna kill 'em or they's gonna give 'em life—an' that's worser."

At a soda fountain we meet the rosy, buff-colored mulatto girl who operates the elevator in a local department store. What about that accident on the road last week? There is nothing to hide now. She looks up from her glass with the stain of dark grapes on her teeth.

"Sure they got him. You see, there was two other folks in the car with him: all colored. He was just seventeen. He was giving the other two a ride. They turned him up to the sheriff. He would of stopped, he said, but he was afraid of a mob. That's good sense. They had his trial yesterday. Ten years. Better'n being lynched, I say."

She is in a hurry. There is going to be a dance. Of course we can't detain her; anyway we would be misunderstood if we persisted in buying her sodas. There are only straight lines in the reasoning of these folks. There is a limit to the number of sodas you may buy a yellow girl on Saturday night. We are too fatigued and depressed to care much.

Upstairs the colored doctors and dentists have offices on the same floor with the black fortune teller who calls himself "Kid Wonder." The latter is away—he has also an office in Birmingham—but the doctors, dentists, and lawyers can be seen through their glass doors. All of them smoke cigars and recline majestically behind their desks. One doctor has an ironing board for an examination table; the wicker bottoms are broken out of the chairs. He has large fan-like hands that he holds before his face as he talks, and we notice that the fingernails wear vivid black rims. A black peasant in overalls and jumper is listening to his words, following his gestures with round-eyed wonder.

We had intended to have a word with the doctor, but we decide not to wait. On the street again. We are forced to admit that the caricatures of Octavus Roy Cohen are less absurd than we had formerly credited them with being. It is interesting that the medicine men and the fortune tellers should have offices on the same floor of the same building, that here these two professions should be inclined to flow together as they did in the middle ages. Let us walk awhile; there is no hurry.

A quick wind blows up a few clouds. There is a brief flurry of rain, then again the small white moon; let us walk awhile. The pool hall is filled with voices, laughter. The barber puts his head out the door and tells us a picturesque bit of gossip about the rosy, buff-colored girl and a certain prominent rich man. He smiles: well, what do you make of it? We do not answer because that is the same question we have been asking ourselves all evening. Again the moon slips into a pocket of clouds.

It is raining when we get on the pike, the windy gusts coming first from one side and then the other. What do you make of it? Certainly there is beauty here, plus quality: the undismayed peasantry, the fruitful land, the many-colored rain, the melancholy of old moss-covered buildings and moss-covered traditions, the crushed and broken soldiers who have never surrendered, much loveliness. But it is all wrong. The beauty of this town is solely the beauty of its sins, its feudal injustices, its peaceful paupers, its colorful hangovers. Cynthe with her bowed head and cupped hand, the giant chauffeur taking pride in his authority as a favored menial, the yellow girl with her purple stained teeth and her flowing ribbons of gossip, the meretricious medicine men, the clean young druggist with his hopeless eyes, the silver-haired rural editor, the strident-voiced stump speaker, the bitter Jewish shopkeepers.

The rain increases. At the turn of the Pike there is an automobile stuck in the heavy mud. We slow down. The white driver beckons to two blacks who are about to pass him without stopping. "Come here boys, give me a push." They do not speak but come quietly and set their muscles against the weight of the car. Presently it gets away. The driver does not pause or look back. No matter. They would not see his gesture anyway. Their caps are pulled over their faces, their heads bowed against the driving rain. Apparently neither they nor the driver have been aware of anything irregular in the episode that summoned them to push a carload of able men out of the mud and left them ankle deep in the spot as the others drove away. Apparently there is no pang, no tragedy.

BLUE BOY

An enormous orange moon was rising over the small plantation world over the tiny rough-board shacks of the Negro quarters, the slim black cottonwood trees, and the old crooked fences.

Little Moe sat quietly on a big whitewashed gate. He had on a pair of two-pocket blue overalls and a red jacket, and though the hour was late his little ginger face was lit by big wide-awake eyes. He had lingered outside in the moonlight because Aunt Cindy, his adopted mammy, was still busy ironing clothes and the house was too warm for comfort.

Moe marveled at the bigness of the moon, at its golden brightness. Beneath it the world looked like a curious little design cut with scissors from dark paper. All the outlines and shadows were plain but there were no colors and no small details. None, that is, except those very near Moe —the whitewashed gate and his own blue and red clothes.

Nearby, the shack door was wide open and Aunt Cindy

was standing in the lighted frame in a bandana kerchief, bending earnestly over the clean white pieces on which she was ironing. With her so close at hand, Little Moe did not fear the night or the black shadows. He could at a moment's warning leave his solitary perch and scoot into the house. Aunt Cindy, on the other hand, was not unmindful of him either. If something should suddenly step out of that dark shrubbery and surprise him, she would be sure to hear him cry; she would be there in a jiffy.

So Moe felt safe out in the cool moonlight. He was not even afraid of the abandoned haunted house across the fields, under its dim solitary trees. To be sure, that was the blackest thing he could see, and everybody in the countryside allowed that it was a most fearful place, but that night it seemed a long way off and even the bats wavering above it failed to terrify Little Moe.

Aunt Cindy finished her work and began carrying the piles of snow-white linen into another room. Later she removed the ironing board and stood in the doorway fanning her glossy perspiring face.

"You Moe!" she called.

"Here me, Aunt Cindy."

"Come on in now and wash your monstrous feet. It's near bed time for lil black boys."

"A'right, Aunt Cindy."

When he had undressed, Aunt Cindy heard his prayers, reminded him of the convenient chamber pot, fixed the mosquito netting carefully over his pallet, and blew out the lamp. Aunt Cindy herself undressed in the darkness. She knelt beside her fresh clean bed in a long white night dress and began mumbling half-aloud an interminable prayer. Long before she had finished, Little Moe was asleep.

The morning was diamond-bright when the child awakened. Young heifers were standing at the white gate, their moist noses resting on the top piece. The little curved road was white in the sun and fruit trees hung over it with dusty, unshaken leaves. Blackbirds were hopping from the trees to the fence, from the fence to the ground.

Aunt Cindy had been in the kitchen a good while. Already the tiny shack was fairly bursting with the fine odors of her fresh coffee and frying bacon, rocking with the rhythm of her singing.

You can weep lak a willow an' moan lak a dove
But if you wanna go to heaven you gotta go by love.

Later, when breakfast was nearly over and Moe was sopping the last biscuit in his molasses, Uncle Primus came up the road driving his white mule to an old two-wheeled cart. He stopped under the shade of a plum tree and began calling Aunt Cindy in great excitement.

"Has you heared it, Aunt Cindy?" he panted, climbing over the wheel. "Has you heared?"

"Heared what, Uncle Primus? What done happen?"

"Lawd, Aunt Cindy, a nigger done broke jail. Boy Blue run off las' night from the county farm. He ain't far from here. And the sheriff's hunting him with the dogs."

"Boy Blue, hunh?"

"Yea. The one with the razor marks, what got life for killin' his ole woman."

"Done bus' jail! Well, tell Jesus!"

"It's a mess. Them dogs galavantin' round here. You better keep the young-un inside till you hears some more news. And if ara you see that rounder Blue, tell him to keep on moving."

"Oh he can't light here, Uncle Primus. No sir, not with them dogs on his trail."

Little Moe had caught the edge of Aunt Cindy's apron. It was not the first time he had heard the old folks discussing the bad Negro with the razor scars. Moe could remember the agitation with which they had so often told the hideous story of how the same Boy Blue had carved his woman to death, slitting her throat. And the thought of the man was more terrible to the child than his fear of the sheriff's dogs.

Uncle Primus' old shoulders were rounded, his heavy whiskers shook nervously. He wiped his face on the sleeve of his red undershirt and climbed back on his cart again.

"I'm gotta press on," he said. "I'm gotta put all the folkses up the line on they p's an' q's. It won't do for nobody to try to hide that rascal now."

"You tell em, Uncle Primus. Tell em all. An' don't forget Sister Mayme what lives in the bottoms."

The little old black man looked grotesque in the bright golden sunshine. His sleepy white mule, tormented by huge bright-winged flies, shook its ears when the old man clucked and began a lazy jog in the dusty path. The overhanging boughs came together as the odd little chariot passed and dust settled on the leaves like powder. Uncle Primus was off to bear his startling news to the other old women and the children.

But a snail could have crawled as fast. Uncle Primus

kept clubbing the hind-parts of his old beast with an air of great urgency, but the pace remained the same. Finally the road curved and took him out of sight.

"Hm. That's that," Aunt Cindy said.

"Yes'm."

"You on'erstan' everthing?"

"Yes'm."

"You gotta stay close by me this morning. Don't get no further away than the gate."

"No'm, Aunt Cindy."

She went inside to her breakfast dishes. Little Moe kept so near her heels that before long she had occasion to regret her warning to him. Several times she nearly stepped on him and before long she was forced to send him out into the yard.

"I can't move for you," she said. "Get on outta here."

Moe left her timidly and sat on the back steps. But his eyes never abandoned Aunt Cindy for a single moment. Something inside him kept fluttering and throbbing against his ribs like a young bird in a cage.

Late that afternoon Moe ventured out to the gate and climbed to his perch on the top. The countryside was painfully still. All the black women and their children remained inside the whitewashed shacks. The menfolks were away working in the rice swamp. They had been gone since the crack of day. A host of birds had settled on the abandoned house across the road, on the broken-down cane mill, and on the shed.

Presently, while Moe sat studying, a lean, wretchedly clothed black man came out of the nearby shrubbery like a stray cat, blinked a moment in the sunlight, and crept over to the gate by Moe. The tall man had a wild, terrified look on his face. He was wearing only a pair of ragged pants and his naked shoulders and arms were scratched and bleeding. He seemed out of breath.

"Whose boy is you?" he whispered to Moe.

"I's my Aunt Cindy's boy."

"Where Aunt Cindy at, son?"

"In the house."

Suddenly Moe noticed the razor scars on the man's face. He tumbled from the gate as if he had been shot, burst into loud unquenchable wails, and scooted into the house.

"Aunt Cindy! Aunt Cindy!"

"Hush that fuss. Is you gone batty?"

"He here, Aunt Cindy? He out at the gate," Moe screamed, his face hid in the old woman's apron.

Aunt Cindy went to the door but she saw nobody. Boy Blue had ducked back into the shrubbery. The road was as still and white as it had been all morning. The fruit trees were quiet and unshaken along the rail fence.

"Hm. 'Magination," Aunt Cindy said. "Like I thought."

Moe looked too. "He gone now," he said.

"You right he gone. He *been* gone."

"I seen him though. He asked me whose boy I is."

"I know. Run long now. You ain't gonna see him no more soon."

A few minutes later, however, Aunt Cindy heard a noise that stopped her own feet in the middle of the room and convinced her that Moe's eyes had not deceived him. The child, trembling again, reached for her apron. There was certainly no mistake now. A pack of dogs was circling about the adjacent fields, coming nearer and nearer Aunt Cindy's shack.

The woman and the youngster came to the door. The sun was down and a thin blue twilight started to sift through the trees. The dusty little road had turned to gold. Banners of wood-smoke stood above the row of white shanties that stretched away in a great semi-circle from Aunt Cindy's. The dogs kept coming.

The sheriff came stalking through the shrubbery with a pistol in his hand, another swinging from his belt. The dogs were still circling, their direction describing an imaginary corkscrew. The sheriff's teeth glistened. He had a twisted mustache and a tall, broad-brimmed hat. He wore high boots and he tramped forward with the terrible directness and menace of a man seen in a nightmare. His teeth seemed to grow larger and larger.

Suddenly, like a frightened rabbit, the ragged black man sprang from a thicket and tore across the open field toward the cane mill and the haunted house.

"No, no!" Aunt Cindy shouted involuntarily. "Not that a way. That house is got hants."

She bit her knuckles at the sight. Evidently Boy Blue did not know the reputation of the place toward which he was making. No Negro had dared to enter those abandoned premises since a day, twenty years earlier, when, according to the report, some mysterious person had gone into the house by night and murdered an entire family with an ax. But Boy Blue was going to enter. He seemed to realize the big house was locked, so instead went directly to the shed beside the cane mill. With a final desperate leap he plunged into that tiny asylum.

He had been inside a few seconds when the first of the dogs plunged in after him. Another second and the next dog followed. Then the next. Seven of them. They went in howling but inside they suddenly became still. The next moment the dogs started coming out, one by one. This time their tails were lowered and they whined and scampered away from the shed like common curs.

The sheriff was a hundred yards behind, tramping with the same somber steps and showing his large, grim teeth.

The shed was silent when he entered. There was a short pause after he went out of sight. Then his pistol barked. And again the place was still.

Aunt Cindy and Little Moe stood in their doorway, stupefied. They watched for several minutes. Neither of them was able to speak. The twilight darkened. Frogs became noisy in the moist grass. Somewhere a guinea fowl was awake. Aunt Cindy's face was wet with a cool perspiration. Her mouth hung open and her eyes were round. Still no one left the shed. The Negro and the sheriff both remained inside. No other sound was uttered there.

Next day the amazing news spread along the cabin row. The sheriff and Boy Blue, both swallowed in one terrible gulp by the haunted shed! The dogs frightened and scattered! It was staggering. These plantation folks were accustomed to miracles, however. They were resigned to them.

Days passed, weeks, months. No one ventured near the ghastly scene of the mystery. Nothing was explained.

Meanwhile weeds grew taller and taller about the place. Morning glory and honeysuckle vines covered the mill and the shed, sealing them tighter each day against the curiosity of Little Moe, Aunt Cindy, Uncle Primus, and the other blacks along the line. Naturally, the story was distorted in the retelling. In time it became a legend in our county.

II

While Little Moe sat on the gate marveling at the early orange moon, John Jason Blue, ironically known as Boy Blue, was lingering near the road with a few fellow convicts, working late. The black men, standing short distances apart, seemed solitary and melancholy in the dusk. The distant buildings of the county farm were in shadows.

Blue's pick rose and fell with a spiritless, clock-like regularity. His mind was not on his work. He was watching the overseer who had wandered a few yards away and momentarily turned his back on his charges. Blue shot a few nervous glances in the opposite direction also. Nearby there was a wood. A bit further, the small Pine River. Suddenly the lean black fellow made a decision.

"Bird in the air," someone shouted.

Instantly all the convicts fell down on their bellies. This had become the cry of every convict who attempted a breakaway; it was a signal for the others to duck and thereby save themselves from bullets that were certain to be aimed at the fleeing one. It was a common alarm—a gesture of honor—for the convict who sounded it multiplied his own peril in order to diminish the risk to his companions.

The overseer, too, heard. He wheeled sharply and saw

Blue zigzagging through the deep twilight. He raised his gun and banged twice. Blue kept zigzagging across the fields. Guards came running down from the buildings. They did not follow far. They could not leave the rest of the convicts.

The men on the ground rose from the dust. The disappointed guards came across the road with their guns. The bird had escaped.

This Blue was a natural-born rounder. In town, on the alley where he was born, the black folks had early predicted a bad end for him. He had been a sullen, morose boy, fond of low company, touchy as a porcupine, as dangerous as a copperhead. He was a fool with a knife. As a youngster, he was searched by his old mammy every time he left the house. Usually she pulled a blade of some quaint description—a butcher's knife, a razor, or a pair of scissors—from his pants' leg or his sleeve.

At the age of twelve Blue cut one of his playmates. At fourteen he drew a knife on the schoolteacher. At sixteen he stabbed a man in a crap game. And at eighteen he carved a rival about a woman. Since then he had put his mark on more than he could remember.

There was a strange, mad artistry in Blue's use of a blade. He could split a hair. He could whip a weapon from his clothes faster than the eye could follow. It was a skill approaching slight-of-hand. His thrusts were sudden, catlike, and deadly. In all other movements Blue was slow and blundering. Anger transformed him, made him a demon.

Eventually this proved his undoing. Blue got a woman who was as bad as himself, a tall woman whose outstanding feature was her purple gums. Unarmed, the two were a close match. Once Blue slugged her with his fist and in return got his face clawed. He never punched her again.

"A man is crazy what busts up his two good fists on a no-'count woman," he observed. "If ever Zelma fool with me agin, I'm gonna take me a ax and flail her brains out."

But Zelma was not afraid. She continued to misbehave. She was smitten on a guitar-playing drifter from beyond the railroad tracks. Blue saw the biggity bare-headed black shuffling in and out of the alley with his box, loafing in front of the greasy little eating place, and finally leaning against Zelma's window, chewing the rag. When he saw Blue, the fellow rubbed his small black dome foolishly and ambled on.

Inside, Zelma gave Blue some unpleasant talk; she became insolent and sassy. When he slapped her down, she got up, grabbed a meat cleaver, and flew at his face. To defend himself, Blue was obliged to use strong measures. Consequently he was now working on the state farm, convicted of murder. The judge had ordered him to stay there till hair grew on his teeth.

After a few years the keepers made the mistake of pampering Blue. They appointed him a trustee. He still wore stripes but he was relieved of the ball and chain. This coddling spoiled him. Blue became restless; he itched for complete freedom. He thought of himself as working for a blue-gummed woman, and he resented the ignominy. When he could endure it no longer he made the break.

Beyond the range of the guns, Blue tramped indefinitely through the turpentine woods, slipping nervously from shadow to shadow. He knew at first that he was being followed. Bullets had ripped the ground near his feet, others had whistled overhead. Later the wood became so full of its own sounds that he was unable to say whether or not the guards had turned back. An odd primal instinct told him to hug the trunks of trees, to keep within touching distance of them. There remained, in the back of his mind, the curious feeling that he might have to climb one of them.

Suddenly the wood ended and Blue, still running, emerged like a harried animal from a thicket. Here in the open he could see the full moon, incredibly big over the trees, illuminating the small black world. For the first time he felt sure that his pursuers had turned back. The air was good, the smell of the sod sweet. Blue experienced a brief, fleeting exuberance in his body, a lightness on his feet, as if he were suddenly no more substantial than a shadow.

He was now crossing a level field with only a vague sense of direction. Pine River, a tiny stream, was somewhere ahead. He knew that he could not miss it. His mind began to work once more. Several problems confronted him. He must get rid of his prison stripes before daybreak. He must also swim the river before morning, for the authorities would be after him with the dogs. But most important of all, he would need to find a chicken yard through which he might pass. That was the sure way to put dogs off your track—rub your shoes in the filth and droppings of a chicken yard.

Blue came to a road, a dusty wagon path that seemed white and shiny in the moonlight. After the pine woods and the rugged uncleared fields, this way was a pleasure to travel, a refreshment to his feet and a security to his mind. He could see the features of the countryside as distinctly as by daylight. The road curved gradually, ascended a small rise and then came down a broad slope. The moon was now directly at his back, touching the earth at the head of the road. For a moment it was as if the bright path led directly from that orb to this, as if Blue had come down that way.

Blue discovered that he had unconsciously slackened his pace.

"Can't do that," he muttered. "Can't let no grass grow under my feet this night. No siree. Got to keep on picking them up. But if I ever gets across that river an' rubs my feet in somebody's chicken yard, it's gonna take the old devil hisself to catch me."

Blue had not figured that the river was so far away; by the road he chose, it had taken most of the night to reach it. He sat a few moments beside the water to rest. The sky was black but the horizon trembled and he knew that dawn was coming. Presently he fastened his heavy shoes together by their strings, swung them across his shoulders, and splashed into the stream.

On the other side he came almost immediately to a row of little crooked houses. In the back yards there were chicken coops and clothes lines with odd neglected pieces of washing still hanging.

"This my place. Here is everything I needs."

He snatched an old pair of wrinkled and shrunken pants from the line. He searched for a shirt but found none.

"Hell with the damn shirt. These here pants is clothes enough for me."

He hurried back to the water's edge, changed his garment, and tossed the striped thing into the stream. Dawn was coming up fast. Roosters were crowing. Roosters! That reminded him. He rushed to a chicken yard behind one of the shacks, unfastened the gate, went inside, and began rubbing his feet on the ground. The chickens were awake. Some of them heard Blue and cackled fearfully in their coops. A large, shadowy dog crawled from beneath one of the houses and came bounding out to the chicken yard with loud tame barks.

"Shucks!" he said. "You ain't nothing but a old hongry house-dog. Get on away from here, pup, before I paste you one. Go on back and sleep some more."

The dog drew nearer and licked Blue's shoes. Then it turned again and trotted toward the shack. A second later a light flared in the window.

"Ah, ah! Let me get going. Somebody's getting up. Think I's aiming to steal. Not this time, peoples. I ain't studying chickens, folks."

He plunged like a wild animal into the shrubbery of the fields that stretched away behind the row of shacks. Leaping from bush to bush and crawling on his belly where the clumps were low, he pressed blindly ahead. The dawn rushed up.

All that morning Blue hid beneath the green clumps of the countryside. He became thirsty and hungry. The saliva in his mouth tasted like brass. His nerves tightened; his senses grew unnaturally sharp. Creeping slowly, he made his way toward an old barn beneath a giant tree.

There he rested, lying face downward on a pile of dirty straw. The barn was unoccupied.

Later, as his gaze swept the small circle of the horizon, Blue caught sight of a row of low-roofed cabin tops. Freshly whitewashed, they stretched away in a long curve. Fruit trees grew around them like a thicket and smoke curled upwards from their little wood fires.

Blue sat on the filthy straw, his elbows resting on his propped-up knees, his long hands dangling between his legs. He was too exhausted to raise his head, but his large round eyes kept rolling in their sockets. He was conscious of no immediate danger, there was no indication that he was being pursued, yet he felt an overpowering need to reach that cabin row. There, beneath the low trees, it seemed so safe and restful. Blue rolled a moment on the straw, stretching his kinked muscles and then pulled himself up and set out resolutely through the fields.

It was late afternoon when finally he saw the black child sitting on the big gate near the first cabin. Blue's heart filled up with happiness at the sight of the youngster. Naturally he was hoping for a place of refuge when he came up and began talking to Moe, but he was even more anxious simply to find someone with whom to talk. The thought that now terrified Blue was that he was alone and friendless, that he was beating aimlessly across the country and getting nowhere.

When Moe burst into tears, Blue's heart sank. Blue felt hurt. He slipped back into the bush and began crawling again beneath the shrubbery on his hands and knees. He moved steadily but without haste. Something in his mind began to flicker, something that turned first black then white. Blue stopped. His breath, going and coming in heavy gusts, whistled through his teeth. He put his head beneath a small bush and fell asleep.

He woke up suddenly and leaped to his feet. The approach of the dogs had sounded through his strained senses as if they were nearer than actually they were. He had thought that they were within snapping distance but when he got his bearings he saw that they were still a hundred yards away.

"Here is where I sells out," he said. "Here is where ole man Blue gotta get up an' shout."

His eyes fell upon the abandoned farm house and the shed. The sounds of the dogs roared in his ears like a strange thunder. He was tearing blindly through the thickets and cornfields. But he did not tire now, he did not feel hot or perspire. Instead his skin burned as from pricks. He curiously imagined that he was gaining on the dogs. At last he plunged into the small shed beside the cane mill.

In the same instant an incredible thing happened to Blue. His nerves, tense and alert following the experiences of the past night and day, seemed to transform impressions. To his senses, strained to needle-point sharpness, all dimensions seemed suddenly altered. The things he saw appeared abnormally large. Due to his lightning reflexes, movements seemed ridiculously retarded. For example, he saw the dogs coming across the yard in long, slow-motion leaps. They looked as big and as cumbersome as horses. Blue had time to grab a rusted corn knife that lay on the ground.

"Hound dog, you ain't got a look-in," he sneered. "You is messin' with Big Boy Blue now. This here is the nigger what can split a hair with a blade. This is Boy Blue what you reads about."

Blue crouched in a corner, his blade lashing out like the arm of a terrible cat. One by one he sliced the crying dogs. One by one they dropped their tails and fled. There wasn't much fight in them.

Suddenly the sheriff's teeth flashed in the doorway, his gun rose. Blue, waving his blade like a maniac, leaped desperately at the armed man. *Root-atoot-toot.* The shots went into Blue's belly. He pitched face downward in the middle of the room.

But already the sheriff was curled in a corner, the corn knife sticking from between his ribs.

MR. KELSO'S LION

Percy always hated to close his eyes. At home in bed he kept them open till the lids were so heavy they just dropped shut, and it was the same on the bus when he and his grandpa went to visit Percy's great-aunt. As usual, he was grumpy when he woke up next morning. It annoyed him to see Grandpa looking so cheerful.

After a while the old man began talking. "Back where we came from—"

Percy squirmed impatiently. "Don't talk to me about where we came from, Grandpa," he interrupted. He paused, ashamed of the way he had spoken, and then added, "I want to hear about where we're going."

"Go back to sleep," Grandpa said. "I don't talk to no sleepyheads."

The bus was rolling along at a good speed. The sun was shining, and most of the passengers had straightened up their seats. The road was smooth. Red embankments ran along beside it, and beyond were fields of cotton.

Wherever there were tractors moving, little clouds of pink dust rose from the fields.

"I'm glad they gave us a seat in the middle of the bus," Percy said suddenly. Grandpa nodded. "It's nice this way. Now we can look out the window at the scenery."

"When do we get where we're going?"

"Just hold your horses. We'll be there soon enough."

"I can't wait to see Aunt Clothilde."

"We'll take a taxicab when we get off the bus," Grandpa chuckled. "I like to travel in style. Makes me feel like *somebody*."

Percy smiled. "I'm much obliged to you for bringing me."

"It's your birthday, ain't it? If I didn't bring you on this trip, I'd've had to buy you a present. Else I'd never heard the last of it. Neither from you nor your maw."

"You're just making fun, Grandpa, but I'm much obliged anyhow."

"All of that's Alabama you're looking at out yonder."

"I didn't notice when we crossed the line."

"You was asleep. It was way back," Grandpa said.

The bus continued to make good time, and in another hour it rolled into Sidonia and stopped at the bus depot. Nobody was there to meet the boy and his grandpa, but the old man knew where he was going, and the taxi driver got them to the house in a few minutes. While Grandpa paid the fare, Percy took the suitcases to the door. Grandpa brought a potted plant in his arm.

Odors of coffee and frying bacon came out of the door when Aunt Clothilde opened it. With loud and happy exclamations she hugged her brother and Percy and led them into the front room and then back into the kitchen.

"You're in time for breakfast," she said. "I'm celebrating today, so I slept late. All I have to do is set two more places. Bless your hearts, I sure am proud to see you this morning—both of you."

"I started to come by myself," Grandpa said with a mischievous twinkle in his eye, "but I got to thinking about my partner here—twelve years old, you know."

Aunt Clothilde laughed loudly. "Hush, Amos. You ain't fooling nobody. You wasn't fixing to come here without Percy. Everybody knows he's your heart. He's mine, too," she added, hugging the boy again. "Put your things down and get washed up. I'll be ready for you at the table directly."

"Here's something we brung you," Grandpa said, handing her the potted flower.

"It's mighty pretty. Set it on the table, and I'll look at it whilst you're getting ready."

"What are you celebrating, Aunt Clothilde?" Percy asked as he returned to the kitchen and took his place at the table a few minutes later.

"My birthday," the old woman beamed. "You and me is twins—born on the same date. Ain't nobody ever told you that?"

"Sure I told him," Grandpa said, overhearing them as he returned. He stood in the doorway a moment cleaning his spectacles with soft tissue paper. He put them back on and took the seat across from his sister. "He musta forgot."

"I remember now," Percy assured him. He gave Aunt Clothilde a big smile as he added, "Happy birthday."

"You and me both," she laughed. "We'll have cakes and candles this evening."

Aunt Clothilde began asking Grandpa questions about their other relatives and telling him about herself. Percy listened quietly while they brought each other up to date on the happenings. While Grandpa admitted that he sometimes got lonesome and Aunt Clothilde could not deny that it irked her not to be able to walk long distances or work in the yard as much as she used to, both seemed to feel they had much to be thankful for and that they were doing as well as could be expected. Certainly there was nothing wrong with Grandpa's appetite, and the little miseries that Aunt Clothilde mentioned did not slow her down when it came to going back and forth between the stove and the table, pouring more coffee in Grandpa's cup and bringing hot biscuits to Percy.

When neither of them could eat more, Grandpa drew his chair back and filled his pipe. Percy got up and began clearing the table.

"I see he's been well raised," Aunt Clothilde commented.

"He's used to helping his maw," Grandpa said. "Being the onliest one she's got, he was obliged to learn how to do things."

Percy had an empty cup and saucer in one hand and was about to say something in reply when suddenly he heard a savage roar outside somewhere. It surprised and frightened him, and it was all he could do to keep from dropping the cup and saucer. For a moment he stood speechless. Never before had he heard such a terrifying sound.

"Is there a circus in town, Aunt Clothilde?" he asked, trembling.

"Not as I knows of," she answered.

"I thought I heard a lion roar," he added.

"If you ain't deef, you did," she giggled.

Still puzzled, Percy stammered, "Grandpa, you didn't tell me there was a zoo here."

"If he did, he lied," Aunt Clothilde snapped.

Percy looked hurt. "Grandpa doesn't tell lies. He wouldn't make up anything that's not so."

Aunt Clothilde winked. "He used to when he was a boy. He used to make up all kinds of tales." She turned and patted her brother's hand. "Amos, I thought maybe you was going back to your second childhood."

"I didn't tell Percy there was a zoo in Sidonia," he assured her.

While he was saying these words, the lion roared again. Percy's hands began to shake. He turned his back to the table so Grandpa and Aunt Clothilde could not see how frightened he was.

Grandpa's voice sounded nervous when he tried to talk. "There sure ain't nothing wrong with that critter's lungs."

"It's enough to chill your blood," Aunt Clothilde agreed.

"I never saw a lion, except at the circus," Percy said, just above a whisper. "I knew they had them in zoos, but I didn't know—"

"You and nobody else," Aunt Clothilde interrupted, "and it ain't right. It's a—it's a sin and a shame, keeping that monster here in our neighborhood."

Grandpa blinked behind his spectacles. "I help you to say that. Who's got him?"

"You remember that old sorry Bumpus that used to be in trouble all the time, don't you?"

"How could I forget Bumpus?" Grandpa nodded. "Pop eyes, buck teeth, and just as mean as he looked."

"He ain't got no front teeth left," Aunt Clothilde remarked, as if it were good enough for him. "He's still mean and trifling though, and he'd rather board that monstrous varmint in his yard than go to work."

"You mean it isn't his own lion?" Percy asked.

Aunt Clothilde explained. "We wouldn't have to put up with it if the lion belonged to Bumpus. We'd find a way to make him get rid of it. But Bumpus just boards the thing for Mr. Stacey Kelso, and Mr. Kelso lives on the other side of town."

Percy finished clearing the table and began washing the dishes in the sink, but his mind wasn't on what he was doing. "I hope Mr. Bumpus keeps his lion on a good stout chain," he said after a pause.

Aunt Clothilde shook her head slowly. "That lion ain't chained," she sighed. "And a good stout pussycat could break out of the cage they got him in." She rose from the table and went to the window. "I expect him to break out of it one of these times," she added, half smiling.

"Could we go around there and see the lion?" Percy asked, excited.

"You and your grandpa can go," Aunt Clothilde said, "but I've seen all I ever want to see of him. Besides, I got things to do. Birthdays don't come but once a year. Move aside now and let me finish the dishes.

After the two loud roars that Percy heard while clearing the table, the lion had fallen asleep in the warm sunshine. He was stretched out with his eyes closed when the boy and his grandfather came into the yard and inched their way toward the cage. Apparently he had also eaten well. Bones were scattered about, some of them with bits of meat left on them. Flies swarmed everywhere.

While Percy and Grandpa stood watching, the caretaker shuffled around from the back of his house. His clothes were patched and ragged, and his face was covered with whiskers.

"Howdy, Bumpus," Grandpa said. "Don't you remember me?"

"I never seen that boy before," Bumpus growled.

"Don't reckon you did," Grandpa answered. "He's my partner—my grandson."

Suddenly Bumpus's face split open with a wide grin. "I ain't had a bit of trouble with boys since I been keeping this lion. Not a bit. He-he! I don't even have to run them out of the yard or tell them to stay away from the cage. I'm getting along fine now."

"We just stepped in the yard to have a look," Percy apologized. "We'll be going now."

"Ain't you scared to keep a monster like that around the house?" Grandpa asked as Percy began to tug at his arm. "That cage ain't nothing but chicken wire. He could break out of that thing quicker than you could break out of a paper bag, if he was a-mind to."

"He might could, but he wouldn't," Bumpus sneered. "He's tame."

"Come on, Grandpa," Percy urged. "The lion might wake up."

"Mr. Kelso raised him up from a pup," Bumpus added. "He brought him back from Africa when he went hunting there with his wife. He's crazy about this lion. You ought to see the kind of meat he sends here for him. Nothing but tenderloin and T-bone. Sometimes I cut off a piece and cook it for myself. It's mighty fine meat."

Grandpa was letting Percy pull him out to the street, but he couldn't help warning Bumpus as he left. "You better make sure that critter don't mistake you for a T-bone steak one of these days. You wouldn't want to wake up and find your own bones scattered around the cage like that, would you?"

Bumpus roared with laughter. "That lion knows me. I'm his friend. He wouldn't hurt me. I could go in that cage and pet him."

"I wouldn't, if I was you," Grandpa called back as he and Percy walked in the other direction.

"I don't think I'd like to live in this town," Percy said a few moments later.

Grandpa shrugged his shoulders. "I wouldn't say that. It used to be right nice here—without that lion."

"Let's keep on walking," Percy urged.

Grandpa didn't mind. He had always enjoyed walking, and today it felt good to him to stretch his legs after the long bus ride. It pleased him to point out to his grandson some of the places where he had played when he was a boy and other places where the neighborhood and buildings were new and different.

The courthouse square had not changed much, however, even though many of the buildings that faced it from across the street had just recently been built. The Confederate cannon and the Confederate monument still stood on the courthouse lawn. Country folk with nothing much to do while in town still loitered around the square. They stared at Percy and his grandpa, and Percy found himself pulling at Grandpa's sleeve again.

"I don't know why you're in such a hurry," Grandpa complained.

"I'm not in a hurry. I just want to keep walking," Percy answered.

"Well, it ain't good to walk so fast when the sun's hot."

Percy slowed down. "All right, Grandpa. We can take our time."

At the next corner Grandpa said, "We'll turn on this street because it goes to the river, and I like it down there."

But Percy kept looking straight ahead. "What's up there on the hill?" he asked.

"That's Angel's Rest," Grandpa smiled. "You might call it Sugar Hill—nothing but fine houses and rich folks. Do you want to see it?"

"Not today," Percy said, turning slowly. "I believe I'd rather see the river first."

Aunt Clothilde was on the porch fanning when they returned.

"You took your own good time," she said.

"We walked all around," Percy told her.

"Well, how did you like the lion?"

Percy frowned. "The place smelled bad."

Grandpa agreed. "But I could put up with the bad smell

if I was sure that chicken-wire cage would hold the varmint," he added.

"Oh, it ain't safe. I know it ain't safe," Aunt Clothilde repeated.

"Somebody ought to complain," Percy said emphatically.

The old woman wrinkled her forehead. "Complain?"

After a moment's pause her brother wrinkled his. "Complain?"

"I mean complain to the city," Percy said.

Grandpa took off his glasses and wiped the perspiration from around his eyes with his handkerchief. "What city you mean, partner?"

"This one. Sidonia."

Aunt Clothilde seemed interested, but puzzled. "I never heard tell of nobody complaining to a city."

"Sidonia ain't even a sure 'nough city," Grandpa smiled. "It's just a little old one-horse town."

"I saw a policeman when we went walking," Percy said. "There must be some way to get rid of lions in any kind of place where folks live."

"Not as I knows of," Aunt Clothilde said. "If there was, I'd sure do it. I'd get rid of that lion, and I'd get rid of old ugly Bumpus, too."

"One thing we can do," Grandpa mused, "is get out the toolbox and tighten up all the locks on the doors and windows."

Aunt Clothilde laughed. "I don't reckon that beast would try to come in here, even if he was to break out, but I'll get you the tools if you and Percy feel like working. Whilst you're at it, you can patch up that back fence for me, too."

"I'd like to do that, Aunt Clothilde," Percy said.

She led them through the house and into the shed room. A few moments later they were in the yard. When they had replaced a few broken slats in the fence and braced up a post that was leaning, they began making the rounds of the windows and doors. They had done everything they could find to do when Aunt Clothilde met them with a pitcher of lemonade and suggested that perhaps a nap before dinner would make them both feel good. She had already closed the blinds and turned back the covers on the beds in her bedroom, and Percy's head scarcely touched the pillow before he dropped off to sleep.

Somebody was talking to Aunt Clothilde in the front room when he woke up. Percy sat up and saw that Grandpa had already finished his nap and left the bedroom. But it wasn't Grandpa's voice he heard talking to Aunt Clothilde. It was the voice of a woman. When he had washed his face and slipped into his clothes again, he peeped out and saw that the visitor was a younger woman who wore a uniform of some kind.

"Come on in, Percy," Aunt Clothilde called when she heard the doorknob turn. "I want you to meet Miss Purify. Miss Purify is the visiting nurse from the city," she added as he came nearer.

Percy bowed politely. "Good evening, ma'am."

"Hello, Percy," Miss Purify said, shaking hands. "Your aunt and I are good friends. Whenever I come to visit her, we just talk and talk. That's why I try to make my visits late in the afternoon. I know I'll never get away till it's too late to make any other visits."

"What was that you said about the city?" Percy asked, remembering the earlier remarks of Aunt Clothilde and Grandpa.

"I'm a public health nurse," Miss Purify explained. "Sometimes folks just call me a 'city nurse.' "

Aunt Clothilde put her arm around Percy's shoulder. "You got to mind what you say to this here young one," she laughed. "His grandpa told him Sidonia wasn't nothing but a little old one-horse town, so now he's holding us to it."

"That's all right, Percy," Miss Purify smiled. "You've got the right idea." She looked at her wristwatch. "I suppose I'd better be moving on now. It's almost suppertime."

"Why don't you just stay and have something with us?" Aunt Clothilde suggested.

"That's sweet of you," Miss Purify said, "but I'm sure you wouldn't have room. You already have two visitors."

"What are you talking about?" Aunt Clothilde sang out at the top of her voice. "I got a table that opens up. I can put another leaf in it. Besides, this is my birthday—mine and Percy's, too. We're celebrating. You just sit right down in that chair till I call you. Percy, I wonder what's keeping your grandpa so long. Go down the street to the grocery store and see if you can't hurry him up. I sent him to get some more candles. I got twelve on your cake all right, but sixteen don't look like enough on mine. Your grandpa thought I ought to have at least twenty-one."

They all laughed.

"I'll stay if you insist," Miss Purify said, "but I won't

sit down while you work. I'm going to help you set the table."

The two women went into the kitchen laughing as Percy hurried out to find his grandpa. The sun was down. Shadows were stretching across the quiet street. Leaves moved, and Percy could feel that the air had become cooler. Workingmen passed him as they rushed home to supper. Some of them were smiling. Others were whistling as they went by. They seemed almost as happy as if it were their birthday, too.

Percy passed a few storefronts but did not pause to look in any of them at first. But when he did not find Grandpa in the grocery store, he began looking in other doorways the old man might have entered. A few moments later he found his grandpa playing checkers with a shoeshine boy in a barber shop. Percy went in and tapped him on the shoulder.

"Did you get the candles, Grandpa?" he asked.

"Go 'way, boy. I'm winning this game," Grandpa answered, brushing him aside.

"Aunt Clothilde sent me to get you," Percy insisted. "She's waiting for the candles. She's got company waiting."

Grandpa looked up from the checkerboard. "The candles? That's right. I knew there was something I was aiming to get from the store, but when I saw this boy in here with this checkerboard, I just plain forgot."

While Grandpa was speaking to Percy, the shoeshine boy jumped two of his kings, so the old man decided there wasn't much need to continue the game. He got up, put his hat on his head and went with Percy to the grocery store. By the time they returned to Aunt Clothilde's house, the table was set, and there was still another visitor in the front room.

"What took you so long, Amos?" Aunt Clothilde asked as Percy and his grandpa entered.

Grandpa fumbled for an answer. "I got detained," he said, glancing at the strange man on the sofa.

Percy decided not to tell on Grandpa. Instead he nodded and added, "That's right, Aunt Clothilde. He was detained."

She rolled her eyes. "I can right well imagine *how* he got detained, but never mind that now. Let me make you all acquainted with my pastor, Rev. Workman."

The preacher, who was almost as old as Grandpa, stood up, and they shook hands. "I stopped in to wish Mrs. Beavers many happy returns, and she wouldn't let me go."

"No, we ain't fixing to let him go," Aunt Clothilde agreed. "We're keeping him here for dinner. Birthdays don't come but once a year."

Grandpa gave the candles to Miss Purify and she started arranging them on Aunt Clothilde's cake. "This won't take but a minute," she said.

"You can all come to the table now," Aunt Clothilde announced. "The dinner's ready. Just sit anywhere."

They found places, and Rev. Workman said a grace that was like a little song. A moment later Aunt Clothilde went to the stove and returned with a steaming platter of short ribs with potatoes around the edges. She placed this near one end of the table and then returned to the kitchen for the platter of green vegetables for the other end, and everybody began talking about how fine her cooking smelled.

Percy's plate was served and he had just taken the first

bite when suddenly the lion roared again. The windows rattled. Everyone in the room became silent, looking at one another in a strange way. Only Percy seemed really frightened, however. Aunt Clothilde looked at him kindly and said in a soft voice, "Don't look so upset, Percy. That old lion roars two–three times every day. You gonna have to get used to it just like the rest of us."

Rev. Workman and Miss Purify began eating as if nothing had happened. Grandpa and Aunt Clothilde kept their eyes on Percy. These three seemed to be waiting. Pretty soon the lion roared again, longer and louder than the first time. Even the two visitors looked up from their plates.

"He must be hungry," Rev. Workman said, trying to smile.

"If he's as hungry as he sounds," Grandpa giggled, "he could swallow up this whole house with all of us in it."

"Let's just hope he doesn't get any funny ideas," Miss Purify smiled. "I can understand how Percy must feel. I get the shivers sometimes myself when I hear that lion. There ought to be a law against keeping a wild beast in a neighborhood like this."

The others began to eat again, but Percy could only nibble at the edges of his food. "What would happen if somebody reported it?" he asked suddenly.

"Who would you report it to?" Aunt Clothilde asked. "The dog catchers?"

"I don't think there's any place in town where you could go to report something like a lion," Grandpa muttered.

"I was thinking that maybe the police would know what to do," Percy said.

The older folks just wrinkled their foreheads. When they finished eating, Aunt Clothilde lit the candles and she and Percy blew at the same time. Both became entitled to get their wishes as well as the first slices of their cakes, but Percy was more puzzled than happy when it was all over and the visitors said good night. When he went to bed, he did not fall asleep for a long time.

"Keep the windows and doors closed this morning," Aunt Clothilde said as Percy washed his face and hands. "There's a breeze blowing from across the back yard, and it smells pretty bad."

"The breeze smells bad?" Percy asked, surprised.

The old woman put her hands on her hips and laughed. "There you go again. I reckon it ain't the breeze but what the breeze brings that smells. It comes from that lion's cage. Bumpus don't never clean it out. The lion can't eat all the meat Mr. Kelso sends out here for him, so it just lays around in the cage and spoils. That's how come the place smells so bad."

"I don't believe I noticed the smell yesterday," Percy said, drying his hands.

"The breeze was blowing the other way," Aunt Clothilde explained.

Percy went out to the front of the house where his grandfather was sitting on the step smoking his pipe. "Can you smell anything out here, Grandpa?" he asked.

"I did at first," Grandpa said. "That's why I'm smoking so hard. This old pipe of mine is powerfully strong. When I'm puffing on it, I can't much smell anything else."

Percy sniffed the air. "I don't know which one smells

worse. Can't we take a walk somewheres, Grandpa?"

"After breakfast we can, if you're a-mind to, but I couldn't walk very far on an empty stomach."

Aunt Clothilde must have guessed what Grandpa was thinking, because she came to the front door and asked the two to come in and have some something to eat, as she put it. When they were about finished and Grandpa was blowing to cool the second cup of coffee, Percy asked Aunt Clothilde if Miss Purify ever mentioned the location of the office out of which she worked.

"I believe it's in the courthouse," Aunt Clothilde said. "Are you aiming to go down there?"

"Grandpa and I might walk down that way."

"Well, if you're thinking about telling Miss Purify how bad that lion cage smells, you can save your breath. She knows already."

Grandpa set his cup down. "Seems like she could get somebody down there to come out and make Bumpus clean the place up and put that spoiled meat in a garbage can with a top on it till the collector came around."

"The garbage collector don't come on that street regular," Aunt Clothilde said. "Besides, Bumpus ain't apt to clean up nothing for nobody unless Mr. Kelso tells him to. Mr. Kelso is his boss and he's the onliest one he will take any orders from."

Percy did not speak again till Grandpa finished his coffee. Finally he asked, "Are you ready to walk, Grandpa?"

The old man nodded as they rose from the table, and a few moments later they were headed toward town, walking along the edges of the pavement. The traffic was not heavy, but occasionally a car or a truck passed them. The breeze continued to blow, and every now and then Percy caught another whiff of the lion's cage, even when they were a long way from Aunt Clothilde's house and coming into the business section of the town. On the steps of the courthouse they paused and Grandpa spoke to a man who looked important.

"We're looking for the Board of Health," he said. "Could you tell us where to find it?"

The man pointed up the steps. "Turn left and keep on down the hall till you come to the sign on the door."

Percy began reading the signs on doors as they followed the direction. "Here it is," he said finally.

They went to a desk inside and Grandpa told a woman who sat there what he and Percy and Aunt Clothilde had been saying about the lion and the filth Bumpus had allowed to accumulate in the cage. She sent them to another desk where they talked to a man, and Percy was surprised to find out how much better Grandpa could say things after he got warmed up a little.

"We want to complain, sir," he told the man after leading up to it gradually. "I never heard tell of anybody keeping a lion inside the city limits before, and I was born and raised right here in Sidonia."

The official at the desk looked friendly enough, but he shook his head. "There ain't no law against it," he said, shaking his head helplessly.

"Seems like there ought to be," Grandpa told him.

"You're right about that," the official agreed, "but there ain't."

"The cage smells bad," Percy added. "Seems like it might be—what do you call it?—unsanitary."

"That's a point," the official said, "and we've had some other complaints about it, too, but there's nothing we can do. You see that lion belongs to Mr. Kelso."

"Yes, we know," Grandpa nodded. "We heard that."

"Well, Mr. Kelso used to keep the lion in his own back yard. The neighbors complained just like you're doing now, so he had to find some other place for it."

"The neighbors don't like it where he's keeping it now," Percy said.

"Before he moved his lion out there, Mr. Kelso looked at a map of this town and found out what part is marked 'residential' and what part is marked 'commercial'—that means for business, you know. Where he's boarding the lion now is commercial. The sanitary regulations are not the same there as they are on the other side of town. We haven't been able to find any way to make him keep that cage clean."

"People live there just the same as they do across town," Grandpa argued.

"Just the same, it ain't 'residential' on the map. It's 'commercial,' " the man added with a note of sadness in his voice. "I'm right sorry about it, too. I caught a whiff of that smell this morning, and I know it ain't sanitary."

"There ought to be somebody who could do something about it," Percy said.

"There ought to be," the official agreed. "There sure ought to be. But who?"

Neither Percy nor his grandpa knew the answer, so they had nothing to talk about for a good while after they left the courthouse. They walked up and down a few streets and looked in the windows of the department stores as if they were trying to find something to buy, but they were really trying to decide what to do next.

"I know what," Percy said suddenly.

Grandpa took the pipe out of his mouth as he stopped to listen. "Tell it, Son, tell it. Don't keep me in suspense," he said eagerly.

"Rev. Workman—we ought to ask him. He might—" Percy stopped without finishing the sentence.

"Well, he just might," Grandpa agreed. "Leastwise it won't do no harm to ask. I wonder where he lives."

"We'll have to ask Aunt Clothilde," Percy said.

So they asked Aunt Clothilde, when they reached the house, and she told them how to get to Rev. Workman's house. But he was not at home when they rang his bell, and his wife told them they would find him at a meeting of the Association, which was around the block and down the street and halfway across town again. Percy and his grandpa kept going until they found the place however, and when they went in they discovered that the Association was a group of about a dozen preachers shaking their fingers at each other and arguing about the meaning of a Bible verse that seemed very simple to Percy and Grandpa. It began, *And I if I be lifted up*. To the preachers in the Association this verse seemed more than puzzling because they couldn't agree on what *up* meant. When someone suggested that it might help if they got a Greek Bible and read the verse in that language, they all nodded and quieted down. This gave Percy and Grandpa a chance to ask if they might speak to Rev. Workman for a moment.

Outside they begged his pardon for calling him out of

such a lively meeting but explained what the official at the Board of Health had told them about the lion. They mentioned the bad odor that came from the unclean cage that morning, and before they finished telling it, Grandpa got worked up again. His voice rose and his arms waved as if he were about to preach a sermon himself.

"It's a sin and a shame, Reverend," he said. "That varmint, that critter, that wall-eyed monster ain't fit for the habitations of civilized folks. His cage smells like I-don't-know-what."

"It's not sanitary either," Percy added.

"We thought you might could tell us what to do," Grandpa insisted.

"I sure would if I could," Rev. Workman said. "But it won't do no good to go to the Board of Health. You found that out. It won't help to go to the police either, because they promised Mr. Kelso they wouldn't bother him about his lion if he moved it outside the residential district, like the man explained."

"Folks live in this part of town, too," Percy reminded him.

"Don't I know! I'm one of them," Rev. Workman said. "But the map shows this side of town as commercial. How you going to change the map?"

Somehow Grandpa couldn't feel much interest in the map of the town. "I'd just like to find somebody that could do something about the lion," he said.

"How about the other preachers in the Association?" Percy asked.

"Why don't we go in and ask them?" Rev. Workman smiled. But just as they entered the room, the preachers found the verse in the Greek Bible. One began reading it aloud as two or three others looked over his shoulder. They seemed so interested in what they were reading that Grandpa touched Percy on the shoulder and motioned toward the door.

Outside he said, "No need to disturb them now, Son. They're too deep in study. Maybe we can come back another time." They walked slowly down the street. Percy looked downheartened. "It must be past lunchtime," Grandpa added, trying to cheer him.

"I'm not hungry," Percy said. "I don't think I could eat a bite."

He felt miserable the rest of that day, and as he lay in bed that night he turned and twitched thinking of the lion and the helplessness of the people who did not like living with a wild beast in their neighborhood but could find no way to get rid of it. Fortunately, he thought, Aunt Clothilde did not seem terribly afraid or annoyed. He and Grandpa would be starting home in a day or two, and she would be there alone with her friends. Perhaps she would think no more about the lion than she had before Percy and Grandpa came to visit her.

Presently Percy heard Grandpa breathing heavily and knew that the old man had fallen asleep. Before long he fell asleep, too, but he woke up with a start soon afterwards. The lion was roaring again, and this time Aunt Clothilde's little wooden house shook as if the thundering animal had been right outside and aiming to blast it to pieces. A window that had been propped open with a stick suddenly banged shut, and Grandpa scampered out from under his covers like a rabbit that had been hiding in a bush. Percy stayed in his bed trembling. He was too frightened to move.

"What's got into that critter?" Grandpa yelled. "He must be gone mad, sounding off like that in the middle of the night." He opened the door and called to his sister, "Did you hear what we heard, Clothilde?"

"Of course I heard it. I ain't deaf yet, nor dead either."

Grandpa stamped his foot angrily. "Confound that man and his lion! I don't like to wake up so sudden. It's hard for me to go back to sleep afterwards. I got a mind to put on my clothes and go round to Bumpus's house and tell him just what I think of him and Mr. Kelso and their monstrous lion."

"I wouldn't if I was you," Aunt Clothilde told him.

"Just don't try to stop me," Grandpa answered feeling in the dark for his shoes and pants. "Somebody's got to talk to Bumpus right straight, and if I don't do it while I'm good and mad, I might change my mind."

"Something's wrong with that lion," Aunt Clothilde said thoughtfully. "I never heard him roar that loud in the middle of the night before."

"Well, I'll sure find out what it is," Grandpa mutttered. "If I had me a gun I'd give him something to roar about."

"You'd have to have a cannon like the one on the courthouse lawn to hurt a lion that big," Percy said, his voice trembling.

"I'm not fooling," Grandpa insisted. "This is nothing to laugh about."

"I'm not laughing, Grandpa," Percy assured him. "But I can't stop shaking. Do you want me to come with you?"

"No, you stay here with your Aunt Clothilde. I'll be back directly."

Grandpa had finished dressing in the dark. He went through the living room and out of the front door. When he had been gone a few minutes, Percy got up and opened the window that had fallen. He propped it with the stick and made sure it would not fall again. While he was standing there, he heard people talking in the other houses of the neighborhood, and some of them sounded almost as upset as Grandpa, though he could not understand what they were saying. He decided to wait up and hear Grandpa's story when he returned.

Aunt Clothilde must have been thinking the same thing, because Percy heard her walking around in her room. He decided to slip on his shoes and pants and go out on the front steps. Before he could open the door, however, the lion roared again, and Aunt Clothilde turned on the light and came into the living room. "You better not go outside," she said, her voice sounding a little uncertain and worried. "Something's wrong with that lion, or else he wouldn't keep on roaring at this time of night. I hope Amos comes right back."

"Don't you want me to go get him, Aunt Clothilde?"

She did not answer right away, but after a while she said, "Maybe you'd better, Percy. Amos is so absentminded he might not know when to stop talking and come home. But hurry—and be careful."

"Yes, ma'am," Percy said, going out the door. "I'll hurry, Aunt Clothilde."

The moon was shining, but in every house lights had come on and people were talking. Percy heard a telephone ring in first one and then another of the houses. A moment later a man came running around the corner. Seeing Percy, the man slowed down for just a second.

"You better get inside somewheres," he shouted. "That lion—he's out!"

"Out?" Percy gasped.

"You heard me," the man called over his shoulder as he went out of sight. Percy stood as if frozen. He couldn't make up his mind whether to continue and try to find Grandpa or to turn around and hurry back to the house with Aunt Clothilde. He had not moved when another man darted out of the dark shadows and yelled, "Do you want to get et up by that lion?"

"No, sir," Percy said.

"Well, you better not stay here."

When the second man disappeared, Percy began running. He was at Aunt Clothilde's door before he realized which way he had turned. She opened it and snatched him in.

"Where'bouts is your grandpa?" she asked, frightened.

"I didn't find him," he answered. "The lion is out. I came back."

"I knew something was wrong with that lion. Lord, I hope Amos stays out of his way."

They locked the door and turned out the lights. Percy ran into the bedroom and closed the window he had opened. Then both of them came back into the front room and stood looking out into the moonlight through the curtains.

"What are we going to do about Grandpa?" Percy asked, his voice trembling again.

"If he comes running, we can open the door and pull him by the hand like I pulled you and then slam it shut again right quick," she said.

But Grandpa did not come running. Nobody passed the house in the moonlight for a while, even though Aunt Clothilde and Percy watched with round eyes and Percy's heart thumped. When they did finally see something moving in the moonlight, it was not running and it was not Grandpa. It was the lion coming slowly across the street.

Percy heard his great-aunt breathe a deep sigh. Then he heard her say distinctly as if praying, "Go the other way, please. Don't come in this yard, you monstrous thing, you. Go 'way! Go 'way!"

But the lion kept coming. It sniffed around the doorstep, passed under the window, and went around the house. As it went by, it rubbed against the house but did not stop.

"He's in the back yard now," Percy said after a few seconds.

"If I had a telephone, I'd call up somebody and tell them," Aunt Clothilde whispered.

While she was saying it, Percy heard a siren scream somewhere in town. The sound came nearer and nearer.

"That must be the police," Percy said softly.

"They better bring the dog catchers with them," Aunt Clothilde answered, as if scolding.

"I wish I could stop them and tell them to look in the back yard," Percy sighed.

Aunt Clothilde snapped at him sternly. "Don't get no

such notion, Son. You can't go outside whilst that monster is sniffing at our door."

Percy didn't bother to tell her he had no such intention. Instead he whispered, "I just hope Grandpa is all right."

"If he is or if he ain't, it won't do no good for you to go out and get chewed up," she reminded him.

When the police car flashed by the house a moment later, Percy realized that there were still other sirens sounding in the distance. Soon the trucks of the Fire Department began rumbling by, slowing down, and swinging around the corner.

"You don't suppose they're aiming to squirt water on the lion, do you?" Percy asked.

"Either that or catch him in one of those nets they carry," Aunt Clothilde speculated.

But neither Percy nor Aunt Clothilde found out just what the Fire Department had in mind. The trucks seemed to stop somewhere around the block in the vicinity of the lion's cage, and Percy did not hear their sirens again. They may have gone away quietly after finding out there was nothing much they could do with their ladders and hose and firemen's axes and hats.

The back yard was so full of shadows it was hard to see where the lion had gone, but Percy and Aunt Clothilde went from window to window and watched for long minutes to see if anything moved in the darkness. Nothing did, however, and it was not till daylight came that they saw the place where the lion had forced his way through the slats of the fence, pushing several of them off as he left the back yard and went through the yard behind Aunt Clothilde's.

Percy's heart did not beat quite so hard now, but he was still troubled about Grandpa.

"Grandpa and I planned to go home today," he remembered suddenly.

"Did the lion make you think about it?" Aunt Clothilde asked.

"I don't know," he answered honestly. "But school opens soon. This is the day we told my mom we would start home."

"You won't be able to go if that lion is still walking around and if your grandpa is somewhere where we can't find him. Go wash your face and put on the rest of your clothes. By then it will be time for breakfast."

He did not feel like eating, but he obeyed Aunt Clothilde, and by the time he was dressed and clean, he noticed people passing on the street outside. He went to the front door and looked out and heard a workingman say that everything was all clear now. Another one explained cheerfully, "He went back to the cage by hisself. Bumpus is busy fixing up the hole where he broke out."

Aunt Clothilde came to the door when she heard them talking. "Seen anyhing of my brother?" she called.

"He must be the one that got hurt," the workingman said.

"Lord, I hope not," she moaned. "Who said Amos got hurt?"

"I heard them say *some*body got hurt."

The men walked away, and Aunt Clothilde turned to Percy with pain on her face. "We can't stop for breakfast now, Son. We got to find your grandpa. Come along."

* * *

Both of them ran all the way, but when Percy reached the house where Bumpus kept the lion, Aunt Clothilde was just coming around the last corner. He waited for her, and they went to the door together. Percy knocked.

The first thing he saw as the door opened were Bumpus's eyes. They were round, and the face around them looked frightened. It was covered with big drops of sweat.

"Is he here?" Aunt Clothilde demanded sternly. "Where's my brother Amos?"

"He should have minded his own business," Bumpus answered back. "He came around here to meddle with me. That's how come he got hurt. It wasn't my fault. I'm going to tell Mr. Kelso just how it happened, and he can tell it to the judge in the courthouse if you all try to blame it on me. Folks ought to stay home and leave other peoples alone."

"Hush-up, Bumpus. I'm apt to lose my patience and whip you myself right now," Aunt Clothilde hollered. "Where's Amos? What's happened to him?"

"He's in here on the couch," Bumpus said. "I dragged him in. He was so busy hollering at me and telling me how low-down and good-for-nothing I am, he couldn't get out of the way. That's how-come the lion knocked him down and scratched him up."

"Get out of my way," Aunt Clothilde commanded as she pushed through the door. Percy followed her into the room. Grandpa was lying on his back, breathing hard and muttering to himself when they reached him.

"That varmint tried to kill me," he gasped. "He's a man-eater. He's ferocious. Somebody's got to help us get rid of him."

"Don't try to talk, Amos," Aunt Clothilde whispered. "Wait till we get you home where I can look after you."

But Grandpa couldn't stop talking. He kept muttering, and every now and then Percy heard him repeat, "It's a sin and a shame. It's a sin and a shame."

When they found out that Grandpa couldn't stand up or walk without their help, Percy went out and asked a neighbor with a car to help them. With Aunt Clothilde, Bumpus, the neighbor, and Percy they managed to get the old man into the automobile and out again when they reached Aunt Clothilde's house.

"If you see Miss Purify anywhere around," Aunt Clothilde said to the neighbor as she thanked him, "tell her I'll be much obliged if she can come to my house the first chance she gets. Tell Rev. Workman, too."

"I hope Mr. Amos will feel better soon," Bumpus said looking shamefaced and ugly as he turned away.

"That's all right, Bumpus. Go on home," Aunt Clothilde grunted. When he was out of sight, she added, "You ain't got the sense you was borned with. That's your trouble."

Aunt Clothilde made Grandpa as comfortable as she could and tried to calm him down by talking softly and telling him over and over again that the lion was back in its cage and that everything was going to be all right. The main thing was for him to rest and get a little sleep.

Percy said very little, but he stood nearby and hurried to do everything Aunt Clothilde asked or that he thought of himself. And he opened the door for Miss Purify when she knocked an hour or two later. He also let Rev. Workman in when he came.

By afternoon Grandpa had received so much attention

and heard so many friendly words and good wishes, he no longer muttered to himself. Finally, when he and Percy was alone in the room, he asked what time it was. Percy went into the next room, looked at the clock, and returned and told him it was half past two. Grandpa dropped off to sleep.

When he opened his eyes a little later, he said, "It's time for you to pack your bag and get ready to catch the bus, Son."

"You're not well enough to travel, Grandpa," Percy said as kindly as he could.

"Never mind about me, partner. Your round-trip ticket is in my coat pocket hanging on the chair over yonder. You got to go back home. Your mother is expecting you tomorrow. I promised to have you back in time for school opening."

"I could miss a few days," Percy said. "I could catch up easy."

"Don't talk about no nonsense like that. You can't afford to miss a single day of school, not ever. You got to go off and study and find out how to get rid of this lion. Remember me and Aunt Clothilde is right here around the block from it, and we can't tell when it's going to get riled up and break out again. Somebody's got to help us get rid of that thing, and it don't appear to me that anybody here now knows how. But you're smart, Percy. You might if you study hard."

"I'll do that, Grandpa. I'll do just what you say," Percy promised. He went to the closet, got his bag, put it on the bed and began packing it slowly. Before he finished, he thought of something. "And let me say something to you, Grandpa. I know Aunt Clothilde will take good care of you, and with Miss Purify and Rev. Workman dropping in occasionally, you'll be all right. But when you begin to get on your feet again and Aunt Clothilde sends you to the grocery store, you better not stop to play checkers when she's waiting for you, because I won't be here to go get you."

"You're right about that," Grandpa smiled.

"And you better wait till I get back before you go round to Bumpus's house to give him a piece of your mind again."

Grandpa didn't promise, but he was smiling when Percy finished packing his bag and went into the living room to say good-bye to Aunt Clothilde and Miss Purify and Rev. Workman.

3 PENNIES FOR LUCK

When I was between ten and twelve, our family lived for a while on the outskirts of Watts. It was not our own home. It belonged to my grandmother, and the circumstances that brought us there had not been happy. But it was a beautiful place to live in those days. Alameda Road was a dusty wagon path beside a railroad track that ran from Los Angeles to the harbor at San Pedro. Tall eucalyptus trees could be seen against the sky in every direction, and there was a small group of them on the back of my grandmother's fenced-in property. There was also a windmill, a kitchen garden as big as a small city lot, and more than twenty fine fruit trees, including delicious apples, Satsuma plums, and lemons that seemed to blossom all the time. There was a barn with a pigeon house on top and a barnyard with heifers and horses munching around a stack of alfalfa hay.

Still it was not a full-sized farm like the one next to it on one side or those across the road. It was a country place of only a few acres, and there were several others of about the same size between us and the interurban trolley station called Palomar.

The railroad track was on an embankment, with oats and barley growing wild on the slopes. There were orchards on the farms across the tracks, but next to us and behind my grandmother's place were shimmering fields of sugar beets. Beyond these beet fields directly behind our grove there was a marsh where you could gather white flowers at certain times and cattails at others, if you didn't mind stepping in mud occasionally. It was a good place to be, and I can understand now why my strong, broad-shouldered father, my small and not very strong great-uncle, and I spent so much time out of doors.

My father was not a full-time farmer either. He had lived on a farm as a boy in Louisiana, but he had left it to play a trombone in a band and later to learn a trade in New Orleans. He still loved the country, however, and often said that if he had been able to make a good living down home, he might not have left. Pausing to think about it a little longer, sometimes he added with a sad smile that if he had been able to earn even half as much money playing his trombone in those marching bands in Louisiana as he was paid as a brick and stone mason in California, he might still be blowing music. Just the same, except when money was a problem, he liked the country best. He never had to be begged to come out to his mother-in-law's place to help her and her brother plant and harvest their small fields, to trim fruit trees or, now and then, to cut down a eucalyptus tree when wood was needed for the cook stove in the kitchen.

I would sometimes help at one end of the saw when the tree was on the ground, but the job of stacking the wood and carrying a few logs at a time to the kitchen was always mine alone. While this was going on, the little old great-uncle my parents and I called Buddy could generally be found at the front gate, under the umbrella tree that shaded it. He was fond of this spot. He could stand there for hours smoking his pipe and waiting for something unusual or exciting to come down Alameda Road.

Buddy was seldom disappointed. He knew, as we all found out later, that if you waited patiently, you could see things on Alameda Road that were not often seen in other places. I suppose that was why I spent so much time with him at the gate when I was not carrying wood or working in the garden. I remember how excited he and I became when a stranger drove by in a sulky behind a slim tall horse that seemed to be in training for races somewhere. It ran like the wind and kicked up a cloud of dust that filled the country air for minutes after he had passed.

Flocks of sheep following a bellweather on their way from the harbor boats to the slaughter house in Los Angeles, a distance of about twenty-five miles, were not unusual. Nor was it strange to see cowboys bringing a shipment of cattle to town. But there were also times when wild horses were unloaded in San Pedro and herded down the road in front of our gate on their way to the old Los Angeles Plaza to be sold publicly, and I can remember a time when a younger uncle of mine bought one of these broncos and tried to ride it home. He did not succeed. When we saw him again, he was walking with crutches, his foot in a cast.

More often, of course, the road was quiet with nothing coming or going. Then I would become restless and think about my cousins and friends in Los Angeles. At one of these times, in fact, I became so eager to visit them I found myself arguing with my father.

This was unusual. My father was not a man to disagree with. He was what some people called positive. When he said *no*, he meant it, and he seldom missed an opportunity to remind me of this.

On this gray Friday, however, I refused to accept his no as the last word, and for the first time, as far as I can remember, I got him to change his mind. I waited several minutes, wondering how I could discuss it further without irritating him or causing him to think I doubted his first, positive no. When his eyes began to seem a little less stern, I asked, quite suddenly, "Why, papa? Why can't I go?"

He was really a smart one, my father. He knew what I was thinking, and he had his answer ready. "Your shoes," he said, pointing. "Look at them. How could you go visiting in Los Angeles and walking on your Aunt Ludy's carpets with shoes that look like you've been plopping around in a swamp?"

"Maybe I could—"

"No you couldn't," he cut me off. "Those things will never look like dress-up shoes again, and I haven't got money to buy you any new ones right now."

I could not dispute that. I had tramped around the swamp in them a good many times. I didn't actually believe I could make them look presentable again, but I was encouraged by my father's tone. Again I waited a moment or two before asking, "Suppose I could get money to buy some new shoes?"

My father had to smile at this. He must have thought it touching that I should pin my hopes to something so unlikely. Where could I imagine myself getting money except from him? Certainly I didn't dream that Buddy had any hidden under his pillow or in his sock. If my great-uncle had money, he would not be standing at the gate. He would be in Watts sitting around a table with some of his old-time friends.

My father's voice was kind but not at all helpful as he said, "Well, if you had money, that would make quite a difference. It always does."

I didn't tell him what I had in mind, and I don't think he guessed it.

Several months earlier he and Buddy and I had run into a little bad luck, and the experience had stuck in my mind. Buddy had been the cause of our misfortune on that occasion, as I recalled, but we all knew he had not done it on purpose. Frequently when the grass and wild grain on the railroad embankment looked especially green and tempting, he would put a halter on one of the animals in the barn yard and take it out to graze on the slopes. Holding the end of a long chain, he would stand by, smoking his pipe, till he decided his critter pet had eaten enough of this special treat for one day and then lead it back into the barnyard. He enjoyed doing this, and the heifers appreciated it, but there was one thing that bothered the rest of us. We could not always depend on Buddy to fasten the barnyard gate securely after he returned, and there was one heifer who seemed to be aware of this too. When she escaped without her halter, she was hard to catch. The beet fields gave her soft dry footing and plenty of room in which to kick up her heels.

Such a performance could be quite upsetting to our household. When it happened the last time, my grandmother had been at home. She was standing at the back door drying her hands on her apron. My little sister was clinging to Grandma's skirts, as she had been accustomed to doing since we lost our own mother. Papa, Buddy, and I instantly dropped what we were doing and tried to head the heifer off, but she darted through the yard and made a beeline for the sugar beet field of our neighbor, with the three of us at her heels.

The neighbor who owned the field was not too friendly. Sometimes he nodded or spoke when he drove past our house, and sometimes he did not. He did not take kindly to our frolicsome heifer kicking up the soft plowed ground and scampering among his young plants. And on this day that I was recalling, we tried our best to bring her back before she could attract his attention or do too much damage, but she was determined to make it hard for us. She romped and scuffed and tore up plants for what seemed to us a terribly long time. My father said he was angry enough to hit her with a stick, but of course he didn't. We just kept running, waving our arms and yelling, and trying to turn her toward home. Finally she got tired, and my father held her with one arm while he put the halter around her neck. By that time we were all out of breath, and Buddy was so tuckered he could hardly stand up without leaning on a fence post.

It had been nearly sundown when we got the heifer back in the barnyard. The worst part of the chase had come a few minutes later when my father discovered that in running after the heifer in the beet field he had lost a rubber tobacco pouch in which he carried his money from the pocket of his overalls. How many dollars it contained and how much change I did not know at the time, but the loss had been enough to distress him, and all three of us hurried back to try to find the pouch before night fell. We had walked and searched between the plants and in the rows until it became quite dark and we could no longer see anything.

My father had been too downcast to even talk about the pouch when we entered the house. My grandmother had responded as she usually did when she felt that everything was not just right. She had taken special care with the setting of the supper table, carefully adjusted the wick of the kerosene lamp as she placed it on the table, and waited quietly for us to take our seats. Even so, the gloom on my father's face had spread to the rest of us, and I don't think we enjoyed our food that night.

Shaking his head and wrinkling his forehead, my father had muttered several times, "I can't figure it out. I know that pouch couldn't hide itself, and there was nobody else out there to pick it up. Where did it go?"

"Maybe you'll find it in the morning," my grandmother said. "How much did you have in it?"

"Biggest part of a week's wages," Papa told her sadly.

"Well, maybe when the sun comes up, and you are rested, you might find it," she had added.

We had gotten up with the sun the next morning, encouraged by my grandmother's remarks, and continued to search till we were all tired again, but we had not found the pouch. And we had repeated this several times in the days that followed before deciding to put it out of our minds. The pouch had been given up as lost, and my father and I had returned to the part of Los Angeles in which we lived in order to be near the school I was attending at the time and to the job where he had been working. My sister Ruby had remained with my grandmother.

While my father and Buddy appeared to have erased this whole incident from their minds in the months since it happened, I had not. They may have felt it was too unpleasant to remember, especially during late summer days that were now so delightful on Alameda Road. We were back in the country again, looking after the place and helping Buddy keep the house while my grandmother and my sister visited relatives in Louisiana on railroad passes provided by my young uncle who worked as a dining car waiter, when he was not trying to be a cowboy and attempting to ride broncos home from the plaza. Now that I was restless and had my father's conditional promise to let me go to Los Angeles, I thought of looking again for the lost money pouch.

The field had been plowed and the sugar beets harvested. The migrant workers who had been brought in for this job had gone up and down the rows chopping off the tops and tossing the beets into piles where the wagons could pick them up, and if the pouch had been anywhere in sight, they would have had an excellent chance to find it. My own chances of finding it still there were certainly not good.

Nevertheless I slipped out into the beet field for one more search, this time by myself, in the area where our heifer had scuffed and scampered and led us on such a wild chase. To my complete surprise, I had not been there more than a few minutes before I somehow unearthed with the toe of my foot in the soft soil the old, scarcely recognizable tobacco pouch my father had lost. It had been covered by the plows and uncovered by the wind, and it certainly did not look like anything of value when I kicked it out of the dust. Perhaps the migrant workers, if they touched it at all, had imagined the old pouch contained nothing more than stale tobacco, but I knew better. I came leaping into the house, babbling like an idiot, and calling to my father and Buddy.

My father's eyes rounded like saucers. His mouth dropped open when he saw that the pouch was still stuffed with his paper money, but no words came from his lips immediately. For about as long as he could hold his breath, he stood as if frozen in that position. It was long enough, in fact, for Buddy to come rushing in from the yard. The way I had bounded and yelled and burst into the kitchen could probably have been heard by neighbors as well as by the three of us.

Getting a good look at the roll of paper money, I now understood even better why my father had been so dejected when he lost his pouch. His work as a brick and stone mason was sometimes irregular, and our family had many chances to find out how it felt to be without money between jobs. When he did work, however, his wages were good, and at the time of this loss, his pouch had been full of bills as well as some small change which the rubber of the pouch had blackened when it laid for so long in the open field.

"What's going on here?" Buddy exploded, peeping over the rims of his spectacles. "Sounded like somebody hit the jackpot."

My father pulled himself together. "You heard right, Buddy. Look at this," he said, giving Buddy a peek at the money, "and maybe you'll understand why it hit me so hard when I lost it out there chasing that no-'count heifer of yours last summer."

"Oo-wee!" Buddy squealed. "Who says that ain't money?"

"I sure didn't say it wasn't," my father laughed.

"Well, when do we go to town?" I asked, no longer the least bit shy.

"It looks like you got me where you want me, son," Papa admitted. "Go wash up and change your clothes."

"You got him all right," Buddy sang out, "right over a barrel." He winked his eye jokingly. "That'll learn you not to make big promises to young whippersnappers. You might have to pay off. Arna must have known where that pouch was all the time. I saw him go out there in the field. I didn't know what he was up to, but he didn't wander around. He went straight to it. I believe he could have found it with his eyes closed."

Both of them laughed as they smoothed out the wrinkled bills, but I was more interested in the coins. They had all turned quite black. Only by the size could you tell the pennies from the nickels. I had never before seen coins tarnished in that way, and I remember thinking about them as my father and I walked the half mile to the Palomar station where the interurban electric cars stopped on their way to Los Angeles.

It did not take us long to find a pair of shoes at a store on Main Street near the old Pacific Electric terminal in the heart of the city, and from there we took an urban street car to the neighborhood where my cousins lived in a three-story house of a kind that was already old and going out of style in California. It was a friendly place, and the voices of my Aunt Ludy and her lively children made it seem even friendlier when she opened the door.

After the first greetings my father said, "Arna will tell you how we happen to be here, but I'm not going to stay. I'm going to call on my boss and find out if he has any more work lined up for me. After that, I'll go back to the country." Though my grandmother's place on Alameda Road was no more than ten miles from this part of Los Angeles, all of our relatives spoke of it as the "country."

"Sorry you can't stay," Aunt Ludy said. "We're mighty glad to have *him* anyhow," she added, pulling me inside and turning me over to my cousin Benny, who was near my age, his two sisters, and their little brother.

"Where's Uncle Benny?" I asked, seeing that all the rest of the family was present.

"He just left," Benny, Jr., said.

"He works at the Post Office, you know," Aunt Ludy explained. "He's on the night shift now."

We all sat down in the living room for a few minutes, and I told my aunt and her four children how one thing had led to another, making it possible for me to visit them this evening.

"Good enough," Benny said, snapping his fingers as if remembering something. "Maybe I can have my party now."

"It's *not* your birthday," Sydonia reminded him.

"We missed his birthday," Aunt Ludy told us. "I told him then we might do something next time Arna came to spend the night."

"That's what I'm talking about," Benny smiled.

"Well," Aunt Ludy said thoughtfully, "if you want anybody else to come, you'll have to go around and invite them."

That was all Benny or I needed, and as my father waved to us and started toward the streetcar line, we hurried across the street and around the block and asked several of the youngsters in the neighborhood if they would like to come over and play games and things. It was twilight by the time we returned, and Angelique and her brother Leo arrived soon afterwards. They were children of one of our family's closest friends. Later on Laura and Henry and Claiborne and Ralph came. Alma was brought by her older brother and Alamae by her mother. All of them lived nearby, and some of them went to Benny's school. One or two went to the school that Sydonia and Juliette attended. The room filled up, and we played games until one of the kids from Jefferson High who had often heard him play in the band asked Benny to play something on his trumpet.

Alamae played the piano for him, and when she decided they had played long enough, she stopped and said that now it was my turn to do something. The others seemed to side with her, and they persuaded me to say a long poem I knew about a man who was in trouble because he had a secret he found it hard to keep. He had committed a crime, and in the poem he was pretending that he was telling something he had dreamed. Everybody listened, but I could see that the story made Benny's little brother and his younger sister shudder a little.

Later we all went up to their playroom. But it was not an ordinary playroom. It was on the third floor where nobody slept, and it was filled with old-fashioned, round-topped trunks like pirates' chests. These were filled with clothes that Benny's mother and mine and their sisters had worn when they were young and "courting," as they called it. Some of the girls could not resist trying on some of the clothes. They even found boxes of jewelry.

Sydonia told us that not all these out-of-style clothes and boxes of keepsakes belonged to her own mother and father or mine. Ours was a pretty good-sized family, scattered in all parts of Los Angeles, but only Aunt Ludy had an extra room in which the rest of them could store trunks and clothing and furnishings they were not using but wanted to keep.

There were also many books up there, and I found one with a story in it called "Tol'able David," which I started reading immediately and couldn't stop. Even when Aunt Ludy called up the stairs to say she had something ready for us to eat and to come down to the living room, I stayed up there alone and kept reading "Tol'able David." Here was the story of a boy who was just the age I wanted to be, was in a hurry to be, I thought. I could have stayed away from any kind of party to finish that story, and I did that night. I scarcely noticed when the party broke up and the kids went home.

My father was quieter than usual as we rode back to Palomar two days later. On the way he told me what he was thinking. His work at his trade was beginning to pick up, he said. His boss had talked about some big jobs ahead for brickmasons in Southern California, but some of them were quite a long distance from Los Angeles. He was thinking we might have to make different arrangements for our home life. While my sister could remain with my grandmother for the present, he could not expect Grandma to keep both of us. Besides, there was no suitable school for me within walking distance, and there was no other convenient way for me to travel to and from a more distant school.

For a long time, he said, he had dreamed of sending me away to a preparatory school, if he could make arrangements, but he feared it might be too expensive for him. Now that he had been offered an opportunity to work on the Aqueduct that was being built to bring water from Owens River to Los Angeles and would have to spend much of his time up there in the months ahead, the boarding school for me began to seem like an answer to his problem.

I was not overjoyed. If I could have remained with my grandmother and Buddy on Alameda Road, I think I would have preferred that, but still the idea of going away to school was rather exciting, and I did not complain. I don't know what happened in between, but a few days or weeks later I was sent to a school in a beautiful setting surrounded by orange groves and with mountains nearby. I soon realized it was going to be more fun than I expected. Among the books I found in a small room that was used as a library was one called *Three Black Pennys,* and I nearly jumped for joy when I saw that the author was the same man who wrote "Tol'able David," which I had liked so much. I didn't like *Three Black Pennys* nearly as well, but its title reminded me that this had been the exact number of black pennies in that lost money pouch when my father opened it in my grandmother's kitchen. I decided immediately to watch for blackened or darkly tarnished pennies until I acquired three. These I decided I would carry in my pocket all the time—for luck.

Well, partly for luck. Partly, perhaps, they would be for me a reminder of the days on Alameda Road near Watts, when the eucalyptus trees could be seen from there, before I went away to boarding school and started out on my first journey of discovery. Partly, too, the pennies could remind me of my introduction to the world of adult fiction. I read *The Lay Anthony* and *Java Head* and then a story called *My Antonia* by another author, and they convinced me I was ready for books of this kind. By watching closely and offering to trade new ones for old, I eventually acquired the three black pennies I needed. They jingled gloriously in my pocket for the next few years, and my luck was very good.

Neither preparatory school nor college did anything to spoil it. I wrote a poem and sent it to a magazine in New York when I was twenty, and they printed it a few months later. I was sure my pennies were working. So I decided to go back East and try to become a writer. I am not sure what my father thought of this plan, but he did not stop me, and when I went to the old Southern Pacific station to catch the train on a Sunday afternoon, he was there with Benny and Buddy and several other relatives and friends. It was late afternoon, almost twilight, when the train pulled away, and I still remember how the little group looked, huddled together on the platform and waving. Suddenly I felt a most unusual sadness.

When I came up out of the subway at 125th Street and Lenox Avenue, it was August in Harlem, and a group of youngsters with what used to be called a "kitchen band" was playing music on the sidewalk. It was as if they had come there to welcome me with their harmonicas, tin pans, washboards, and drums. Some of them were dancing the funniest dance I had ever seen. When I stopped to look and listen, they made a circle around me, pushed me in the middle and tried to make me do the Charleston. But I didn't know how, and pretty soon they let me go and went on doing it themselves as I walked away.

But this was enough to let me know that New York's Harlem was a happy place to be at that time, especially if you had three right black pennies in your pocket, as I had, and knew what they meant. Within a few months I won three prizes for poems I had written and one for a short story. I rented a room with a friendly old couple, found a job that wasn't bad, and met girls prettier than any I had seen before—or just as pretty.

One of them caused me to decide that the trip to Paris, which I had often dreamed about while in college, could wait. I married her instead. The money from my prizes we used to rent a small apartment and start buying things to go in it. Even when Harlem began to feel hard times and my job ran out and we went to Alabama and moved into an old dilapidated house that had once been a handsome mansion, I thought my luck was still good—until we found out our "mansion" was haunted. Nevertheless, I kept my black pennies jingling, and when we moved to

Chicago and I still found a job where I could work and earn—though jobs were terribly scarce—I could have sworn my pennies were worth their weight in gold. I would not have parted with a single one of them at any price. But I did.

I did it to help another young writer. His name was Richard Wright, and I met him in the Chicago Loop where he was waiting for a street car but didn't have enough money to pay his fare. He needed two more pennies. I tried to let him have a dollar, but he was proud and wouldn't accept a cent more than the two pennies he needed. I couldn't tell him that these three pennies I had were special. That was my own secret, but he talked me into letting him borrow two of them. He promised to return them the next Friday.

Well, he did. He walked two miles to our apartment and proudly gave me back two bright and shiny pennies, which were no good at all to me. He also read to me some pages from the book he was writing which he hoped would get him started as a writer. And sure enough the book won a prize and started him on a fine career. I think my pennies may have helped him. He and I became friends, but I never told him how being without my three black pennies had hurt my own chances.

It took a very long time to find two more that were really old and tarnished enough to go with the one I still had. Finally I told an audience of young people about this experience and how I missed the pennies I had become so used to carrying. To my surprise, a day or two later, when I opened my mailbox, out dropped not two but a handful of pennies, all very black.

I was writing a story for young readers at the time, and

the pennies must have worked. I still see copies of that story in schools and libraries, and when I do, I remember what went before it. Sometimes, when things are not going too well and I feel discouraged, I am still tempted to reach in my pocket and touch my three black pennies.